CALEB'S WORLD

SLEEP WRITER BOOK 3

Caleb's World

by Keith Robinson

Printed in the United States of America
First Edition: December 2015
ISBN-13 978-1522887669

Visit www.UnearthlyTales.com

CALEB'S WORLD

SLEEP WRITER BOOK 3

KEITH ROBINSON

Chapter 1

Liam Mackenzie would have looked forward to the Saturday night weenie roast if not for the imminent threat of destruction hanging in the air.

"I'm scared," Madison whispered. Just out of earshot, Liam's dad poked the fire and bent to add more logs. "I wish I could just tell everyone the truth and have the place evacuated."

"Wouldn't do any good," Ant muttered. "In fact, you'd end up in an asylum."

It was just a small neighborly gathering, the Mackenzies and the Parkers, plus one other. Liam's parents had come up with the idea, a way to truly welcome Madison Parker, her five-year-old brother Cody, and their parents to the neighborhood. Anthony Carmichael—Ant to his friends—was the extra. The sky was darkening, the fire good and hot, the beef hot dogs unwrapped.

"Who wants a roasting stick?" Mr. Mackenzie asked.

"Me! Me!" Cody yelled, jumping up.

"Careful with that," Mrs. Parker said as the boy grabbed the long, sharpened stick. It had been soaking in a bucket of water for the past hour so it wouldn't easily catch alight when held over the fire with a hot dog on the end. She helped him spear it, and he tentatively waved it over the fire. "Hold it still," she said. "Not *in* the flames— hold it up a bit—that's better."

As the adults chit-chatted, Liam leaned sideways in his chair. "Let me see the message again, Maddy."

Madison frowned. "Not here."

She was all about movie director Tim Burton tonight, wearing a t-shirt with *The Nightmare Before Christmas* characters all over it, and carrying a white-and-grey clutch with the dog from *Frankenweenie*. And clutch it she did.

"Come on, nobody's looking," Liam insisted.

She extracted a folded sheet of paper and smoothed it out on her on lap. Since she sat between the boys, both Liam and Ant leaned in to read it.

6:52 PM. Liam's house. Keep Ant and the rest out.

The curiously specific instruction still mystified Liam. "Why Ant but not Madison and me?" he wondered aloud.

"The message is for me, so it probably wouldn't mention me by name," Madison said.

"Okay, but why just Ant? Why does *he* have to stay away but not me and you?"

Liam knew the information had been sent back by a future version of Madison using an echo wand, whereas his friends thought her curious habit of writing herself messages in the night was just a form of sleepwalking. He wished he could tell them the truth, but eighty-something Madison had warned against it for fear of disrupting the timeline. The echo wand was buried in the yard. Knowing the danger her messages were putting them in—or *would* put them in—what if she destroyed the wand in an attempt to avoid confrontations with aliens? Everything would change. Her future would unravel.

Liam had seen her future as well as his own. But he hadn't seen Ant's. What would happen if his friend defied the instruction and entered the house just before 6:52? The truth was, *anything* could happen. He could die.

There was also Ant's premonition to consider. Last

weekend, while Liam had been off battling Gorvian time grubs, his worried friend had used the echo wand to take a peek into the very near future and check on the state of affairs. Ant had seen himself arriving at Liam's house . . . or rather a hole in the ground where the house had once stood. The house had been utterly pulverized.

Or would be. If the future was set in stone as Liam believed, the question was not so much *if* the house would be pulverized but *when*. Tonight? Was that what the message warned of?

"Why keep Ant out?" Liam said again, shaking his head. "Why not us, too?"

"What are you guys looking at?" his mom called, breaking through the adult conversation.

Liam glanced up to find all four parents looking his way. He and Ant jerked away from Madison and left her alone with the sheet of paper as though it were something distasteful.

To her credit, she refrained from stuffing it back in her clutch and looking even guiltier. Instead she shrugged and waved the paper in the air. "Just getting some feedback and ideas for a story I want to write."

"Oh," her mom said, half her attention on Cody as the boy leaned toward the fire with his slowly darkening hot dog. "Well, come on, let us in on the plot." She gestured toward the other parents. "Maybe we can help."

Liam ground his teeth together. Why did adults have to be so nosy and annoying?

Luckily, Madison kept her cool. "No way. Sorry, Mom. I love you, but this is not your thing at all." She folded the paper and carefully tucked it away.

All four parents laughed and returned to their own

3

affairs, leaving Liam, Madison, and Ant to continue their highly sensitive discussion. "It's 6:35 already," Ant whispered. "Do you think I have time to roast a dog before the event?"

"*You* have time for anything you like," Liam retorted. "You're not going inside the house. You can sit here chewing while Madison and me are annihilated."

"We're not going inside," Madison said firmly. "I don't care what the message says or doesn't say. If something bad is going to happen to the house, we're staying out here at a safe distance."

Liam opened his mouth to argue, to say that time couldn't be altered, that if future-Madison was suggesting her past self go into the house with Liam, then that was exactly what would happen. He decided to hold his tongue, though. There was no point debating the issue. The next twenty minutes would decide things.

Still, no matter how sure he was that the future could not be altered, Ant's premonition had to be a mistake. Everything was quiet right now, the air still and the temperature only a tiny bit on the cool side. It was an almost perfect evening for a weenie roast.

None of that would stop a laser bolt from space, though. Or a meteor. He looked upward, half expecting to see a flaming ball with a fiery contrail heading toward the small town of Brockridge.

"No matter what," Madison warned, "all three of us stay outside. Agreed?"

Both Liam and Ant mumbled their agreement.

At that moment, Ant's driver Barton emerged from the darkness of the lane and caused a break in the adult conversation. "Can I help you?" Liam's dad said, getting to his feet as the dark figure ambled up the driveway. "Oh, it's *you*." He stood and held out his hand. "Barton, right? I don't think we've properly met. Want a hot dog?"

Ant had a frown on his face as the adults exchanged introductions. "Weird," he whispered. "Barton *never* leaves the car and butts in like this."

After a few minutes of small talk, Barton excused himself from the parents and moved toward Ant. "Excuse me for interrupting, young sir," he murmured. "It's nearly time, is it not? And this is something I felt I had to see."

A look of understanding fell over Ant's face, and he turned to Madison. "He overheard me talking to you on the phone when you called this morning. I was heading into town at the time. I might have repeated out loud what you told me."

Madison nodded. "You repeated it once or twice, yes." She smiled at Barton. "I guess we should have let you in on this properly since you have, um . . ." She gestured toward Liam's house, which stood thirty or forty feet away.

He smiled and gave a single nod. "A special interest in this residence? Yes. I hope you don't mind if I join you on this occasion?"

Our gang is growing, Liam thought absently.

"Liam!" his dad barked suddenly. "Don't just sit there. Get the poor man a chair."

"Huh?"

"There's another fold-up chair in the laundry room. Go grab that, would you?"

His mom chimed in. "And bring the glow sticks. I think they're in the closet in my room. Top shelf on the left."

Liam felt a chill. He could feel Madison and Ant staring at him. He even saw, out of the corner of his eye, Ant sneaking a glance at the time on his phone. Liam didn't need to see it to know the significance and the *timing* of this turn of events.

"Don't go inside," Madison whispered.

"Liam!" his dad barked again.

Barton turned and held up a hand. "It's okay, Mr. Mackenzie, I don't need a chair. I've been sitting all day. All a chauffeur ever does is sit."

Liam's dad huffed a laugh while still managing to scowl at Liam. "Well, whether you stand or sit is up to you, Mr. Barton, but you should at least have the choice. Liam! Get the chair and glow sticks."

With Madison and Ant staring wide-eyed at him, Liam shrugged and stood up.

Ant turned his phone around so Liam could see it. The time read 6:45 PM. Only eight minutes until the event.

"I can do this," Liam said, suddenly determined to be in and out in record time. "Five minutes tops. Be right back. Stay here."

He dashed past Barton, who looked on with narrowed eyes. Was he confused by the exchange or eagerly awaiting the outcome?

Five minutes in and out, Liam thought as he tore across the lawn, up onto the deck, and in through the French doors. Ant's vision of a destroyed house ate away at his gut, but his brain suggested he would survive no matter what, because he'd already proved the universe wasn't done with him yet. He'd returned to life *twice* during his recruitment as one of the Ark Lord's soldiers. His own vision of the future featured an elderly version of

6

himself and Madison. He would survive whatever life tossed at him over the next seventy or eighty years.

Still, the prospect of impending annihilation had his heart pumping. How could he survive a laser bolt or meteor from space?

He grabbed the folding chair from the dumpy laundry room first, not caring that he bashed the walls with it on the way out. The room was undecorated anyway.

Next he hurried into his parents' room and yanked the closet doors open. Flipping the light switch on, he stood on tiptoes and ran his hands across the top shelf. Where were the glow sticks? Ah, right there—a whole box of them bought specially for an outdoors party such as a weenie roast. They were for kids, really, and Liam wasn't a kid anymore, but maybe his mom just wanted to light up the lawn to prevent anyone from tripping. It didn't matter as long as he got them and the chair outside pronto.

His fingers brushed against the box, but he couldn't get hold of it. He tried jumping for it, then mentally slapped his head and unfolded the chair to stand on. How much time did he have? He couldn't have been inside more than two minutes, surely? Three at the most.

Placing a foot in the middle of the seat, he hoisted himself up—and the chair's fabric ripped. His foot shot through a hole, and he staggered, grabbing at whatever dresses hung nearby. A few hangers came loose, and he growled with annoyance as he tried to untangle himself from everything.

He thought he heard a door open, and he paused to listen. Hasty footsteps. Then a pause and a whispered voice from the hallway: "Liam? Where are you? Hurry up!"

Madison? What was she doing in the house?

A terrible feeling came over him. The specifics of her message, the timing . . . All of it seemed to be coming together. Which mean the house might very well be destroyed within the next minute.

"Madison, get out!" he yelled, kicking at the ripped chair.

Then again, what if he tore out of the house just in time and then absolutely nothing happened? How would that look to his parents?

He fumbled with the handful of dresses for a second, then threw them down in frustration. *Sort them out later*, he thought. *If there's a later.*

He made a leap for the shelf and batted at the box of glow sticks.

"Liam, get out there!" Madison yelled from the bedroom doorway, her voice much sharper and clearer now.

"I can't reach the stupid glow sticks," he yelled back. "You're taller. Come help me—"

"*Leave* them! We have to get out!"

Liam made one last attempt at grabbing the box and managed to hook it closer to the edge of the shelf so he could get a firm grip on them.

Then he froze.

First he heard a faint whispering sound, then a rumble. After that, a tremor started under his feet. His fingers were still on the box of glow sticks, which vibrated under his touch. He felt the floor twist as the tremor increased. *Earthquake*, he thought with a jolt of terror. Before his eyes, a crack appeared in the wall and drywall dust trickled out.

He heard shouting and Madison calling to him. He glanced toward the window. Although dark outside, there was enough light to see both his parents' cars in front of the garage.

The cars were starting to rise, along with the garage, driveway, and everything else.

Paralyzed, Liam watched with disbelief, his fingers resting on the box of glow sticks on the shelf. Then the floor bucked, and his knees gave out. He sprawled on the floor and just had time to see solid rock moving upward outside the bedroom window before the room tilted violently and he was flung deeper into the closet. The doors snapped closed, and then one came loose and whacked him on the head. At that point the room lights went out, and he was in darkness with an awful feeling in his stomach, the sort of feeling associated with descending in a speedy elevator. He heard Madison scream.

The noise was terrifying: groaning and crashing, the rending of metal, creaking and cracking, and above it all a continuous scraping sound that reverberated all around. And throughout the ordeal, Liam was pummeled by the contents of the closet and slammed back and forth against tilting walls.

Then came a deafening crash. He slammed into a wall, and heavy objects pummeled him in the darkness.

Chapter 2

When Liam woke in pitch-black darkness, he was spread-eagled on his back buried in what felt like shoes and dresses, with a busted closet door pressed painfully against his right arm. He immediately started choking on dust as he fought to extract himself from the mess.

With shaking hands, he covered his mouth and nose with his shirt as he twisted around and sat up. He couldn't shift the broken closet door, so he maneuvered out from under it, flinging shoes aside. He stared blindly into the darkness, wondering how it could be so utterly black. He checked his face with one shaking hand, convinced his eyes had been gouged out. But no, his face seemed fine, his eyes still in their sockets. The dust was making him blink furiously, so maybe he'd been temporarily blinded.

Or maybe the house was buried under tons of rubble.

He breathed hard through his shirt, and finally found his voice. "Dad! DAD!"

No answer. All was eerily still.

"I'm alive," he said loudly. Then: "Maddy! MADDY! Are you okay?"

He waited, listening hard. When he received no answer, fear gripped him again. What if she was dead? Crushed under falling debris or pierced by a rafter?

Trying hard to control his thudding heart, he took a deep breath. She *couldn't* die, because he'd seen her in the future. He had to cling to that. Maybe she was just unconscious.

Speaking of which . . . He fingered a bump on his head. How long had he been out?

His parents had to be clawing their way through rubble to get to him by now. There were probably rescue crews on the way already. Liam knew very little about earthquakes and fallen buildings, but he was sure the structure was unsafe. If he moved around, he could cause something to shift, and the whole roof could fall in on him. He was lucky to be alive. If he hadn't been in the closet, maybe he would be squashed under the bedroom ceiling right now, or crushed against the wall by the bed.

My phone! Eagerly, he fished in his pocket and pulled out his smartphone. Thumbing the 'on' button, he frowned when nothing lit up. If he could only *see* . . .

An idea leaked into Liam's mind. The glow sticks! Where were they?

He felt around, finding shoes, clothing, bits of drywall, splinters of wood, and finally a box. He wished his hands would stop shaking as he jerkily ripped open one end and pulled out a bag. He dug his fingers into it, and a collection of long plastic sticks tumbled into his lap. He grabbed one and bent it sharply. Light flared immediately. He shook it from end to end, and a welcoming green glow began to illuminate the closet.

Then he looked at his phone with disgust. Its glass front was completely shattered, the entire thing bent out of shape.

He tossed it aside and crawled out of the closet to inspect his parents' bedroom in the wan glow stick light. It wasn't pretty. There really wasn't much left to call a bedroom. The whole room had tilted. The walls had buckled and folded, and the ceiling hung low, just three feet off the floor at one end and maybe five at the other. It sagged even lower in the middle because of a split that ran its length, allowing pink insulation to hang down around splintered ceiling joists. It was like a monster's underbelly had been sliced open.

It was staggering how much debris littered the floor. The bed was remarkably intact, though coated in dust. His mom's dresser and chair remained in place, but her giant mirror was obliterated, her jewelry, hair brushes, and makeup lost.

Through the destroyed window, outside in the blackness . . . Liam stared hard, trying to figure out what he was looking at. Again he wondered how long he'd been unconscious. Maybe it was already hours later, the middle of the night. Still, even the blackest of nights offered smudges of light here and there, unlike this suffocating vacuum.

He thought about fumbling his way across the debris to get a better look outside, but something held him back. He wasn't ready for that yet. First he had to find Madison and check the rest of the house. Surely it wasn't *all* as bad as this.

Liam coughed some more as he crawled out of the closet toward the bedroom doorway, which seemed to have withstood the collapse despite the sagging ceiling. He remembered something about people in earthquake zones being taught to get out of buildings if there was time, but otherwise stand in a doorway, which acted as a brace.

Still crawling, he held aloft his glow stick and found his way into the hallway. The laminate wood flooring, which his dad had laid himself, remained glued together in large twisted sections. He peered into the shadowed hall, envisioning rather than seeing the doors to the laundry room and bathroom on his right, his own bedroom on the left, and the lobby leading to the kitchen and living room at the end. He knew those doorways were there in the darkness; he just couldn't see them.

"Maddy?" he said softly.

Thinking of flashlights and candles in a drawer in the kitchen, he headed straight up the hall, staying low, afraid to stand. The ominous creaking and groaning reminded him that the place could collapse again, so he crawled in near darkness, illuminated in a lurid green glow which stretched maybe five feet ahead.

He passed the bathroom on the right and glanced inside. "Maddy? Are you in there?"

Seeing and hearing nothing, he moved on to the laundry room, also on the right. There was nothing of interest except a squarish hole in the floor, a washer and drier, a spilled laundry basket, and a fallen shelf.

"Maddy?"

His bedroom was next, on the left-hand side, and he couldn't help thinking about his last remaining precious things, all of which had escaped being sucked into a wormhole last Saturday: a few favorite science fiction and fantasy novels, his *Star Wars* action figure collection he'd always kept stashed under the bed, his Frodo sword, and of course his laptop!—all most likely destroyed.

Liam called again for Maddy but was greeted only by silent darkness. Gritting his teeth, he crawled past and on to the lobby, then into the kitchen through a twisted doorway. "Maddy?" he said again as he entered and tried to penetrate the shadows with his glow stick.

Still no sign of her.

He edged down the kitchen's sloping hardwood floor and bumped into the cupboard under the sink on the opposite wall. Something crunched under his knees, and he winced and jerked away. The floor at this end of the house was tilted sharply in two directions, but as the green glow filtered into the darkest corners, Liam realized the room wasn't in bad shape all things considered. At least the walls weren't buckled and folded, and the ceiling, though warped, was in one piece. The refrigerator leaned back against the wall. If the room had tilted the other way, the monstrous appliance would have launched across the room.

The door to the garage stood wide open, revealing a black nothingness beyond. The extension, which had been built onto the house many years ago, seemed to have vanished.

Liam sniffed. He smelled gas, but it wasn't incredibly strong. He just had to hope it wasn't seeping into the house. Perhaps it was escaping into the backyard.

Thinking of the backyard, he noticed again how utterly black it was outside the glassless window and adjacent double doors that led onto the deck. He had come in through those doors just a short time ago to fetch a chair; now they stood open with a few remaining shards of glass poking out of the frames, the rest having slid down the slanting floor to where Liam knelt.

He couldn't get his head around what he was seeing outside. Or rather, what he *wasn't* seeing. There was nothing—no light from the moon or weenie roast fire, no stars, no flashlights bobbing frantically as rescuers scrambled over rubble, no strobing blue lights from fire trucks and ambulances. Nothing at all except blackness. And no sound either, just an eerie silence.

Yet the doorway offered a clear exit from the house. Madison had probably already staggered outside, dazed from a head injury. Liam knew he had to follow her out.

He climbed to his feet, discovering for the first time that his left ankle hurt. Come to think of it, his right elbow hurt too, and when he touched it and held up his finger in the green light, there was something dark smeared there. Blood. He leaned against the countertop, his back to the sink, and checked himself over. His t-shirt was torn on the right side where the closet door had pressed against him. He was bruised there, too. The side of his face felt a little delicate as if he'd been scraped by something. His ear on that side felt sensitive, like someone had clobbered him upside the head.

But nothing serious. No broken bones, no gaping wounds.

He pulled open the drawer next to the sink—or rather yanked at it for half a minute until the handle came off, then levered it open with a bread knife. Inside he found the flashlight he had been expecting. He switched it on and dumped the glow stick on the floor.

Then he shone the flashlight outside onto the deck.

And saw nothing but a wall of rock.

Chapter 3

Ant Carmichael couldn't help feeling anxious when Liam disappeared inside the house to fetch the chair and glows sticks. Madison couldn't, either; she sat fidgeting and chewing her lip as precious minutes ticked by.

6:52 PM. Liam's house. Keep Ant and the rest out.

It was already 6:49 PM.

"He's not going to make it," she murmured. "He shouldn't have gone in."

"No, he shouldn't," Ant agreed, suddenly feeling irritated. What was it with Liam? Why did he always have to leap into danger? He could have thought up a dozen excuses to avoid the place for an extra few minutes. Heck, he could have flat-out argued with his parents, obstinately refusing to go inside. Yes, it might have gotten him in trouble, but he would have been forgiven the very instant a laser bolt from space hit the house and obliterated it.

Instead, Liam had thought it better to dash inside and get the job done.

Idiot.

Madison repeatedly checked the time on her phone, her hand shaking. Meanwhile, Barton loitered in the background, clearly aware that something was about to happen.

Abruptly, Madison climbed out of her chair. "I'm going to hurry him up."

Ant jumped to his feet also. "Maddy, don't be an even bigger idiot than Liam. He'll be out in a minute."

"We don't *have* a minute," she said fiercely, waving her phone in his face.

Actually they did. Three minutes remained on the clock. Still, it was cutting it close.

He grabbed her arm, but she shook him off and whispered, "I'm not going inside. I'm just going to yell at him from the door to get his butt out here."

Ant opened his mouth to say that a laser bolt from space wouldn't care if she stood inside the house or in the open doorway; it would still fry her. But she was already hurrying across the lawn.

All four parents had been deep in conversation, but now they looked up. "Where's she going?" Mr. Parker asked.

"Bathroom?" Ant suggested, returning to his seat and trying to look nonchalant.

That simple answer did the trick. They resumed their conversation, unaware of the impending doom. Ant wondered if he should try to move them farther away. Just how big a blast would this laser bolt cause? Would the parents be caught up in it? And Cody was just a small thing. He was standing away from the fire with a flashlight in his hand, pointing the beam directly into his face, a picture of innocence.

Ant grimaced. A laser bolt from space? Maybe he was jumping to the wrong conclusion about this latest sleep-written event. Maybe it was just another wormhole. If so, Liam and Ant might end up being sucked into it, but at least it wouldn't be as dramatic as a massive beam of light incinerating the house.

He watched as Madison climbed the steps to the deck and stuck her head inside the double glass doors. He didn't hear her calling Liam's name, but he guessed she was doing so. Ant reached for his phone and thumbed it on. Roughly two minutes left.

When he looked up again, he had time to see Madison disappearing inside.

"What the—?" he growled. Looking up at Barton, he whispered, "She said she'd stay outside! What *is* it with those two?"

"I fear I've caused a major problem," Barton said, reaching up to remove his chauffeur's cap so he could smooth back his thinning hair. "If I hadn't showed up here, Master Liam wouldn't have been told to go inside and fetch me a chair."

"Or glow sticks," Ant muttered.

Barton leaned forward and spoke in Ant's ear. "Are you expecting something other than a wormhole?"

Any other time, Ant would have been surprised at how much Barton had picked up on. Right now, though, he didn't care what the chauffeur knew. "I had a vision of the house being destroyed by the Ark Lord, but the Ark Lord is dead, so I don't see . . . Look, I might be wrong about this, but Maddy's never wrong about her messages. Something's going to happen. We just don't know what."

"The Ark Lord?"

Ant shook his head. "Evil space villain with a massive prison ship. Liam lured him into a wormhole and then deactivated it. The Ark Lord had no space suit on, so he died."

After a pause, Barton said, "And I take it Liam had a space suit on at the time?"

"No, he was a robot, so he didn't need one."

"Ah."

No doubt Barton was putting several pieces together in his head. He'd seen things but had never been told the full story.

"Where *are* they?" Ant demanded, standing up again.

Liam's dad looked up. "I was wondering that myself. How long does it take to find a chair?"

"And glow sticks," Mrs. Mackenzie said.

Ant took a deep breath. "I'll go look."

As he strode across the lawn, he realized he was falling into the same trap as the others and labelling himself an idiot. This was exactly the kind of scenario he hated in TV shows and movies. Why couldn't characters stay put? Madison had even mentioned him specifically in her sleep-written message: *Keep Ant and the rest out.*

He stopped, clenched and unclenched his fists, took another few steps, paused again, and ended up checking his phone once more.

6:52 PM.

He felt the blood drain from his face. If the event hadn't happened already, it was about to, anytime within the next sixty seconds, maybe less . . .

A sudden rumbling caused him to freeze. This was it. He instinctively looked up, expecting to see a massive spaceship descending from the evening sky, or perhaps the creepy shadow of it blocking the stars, or maybe even just a fiery ball of destruction plummeting toward him. He saw nothing, but the rumbling quickly grew louder, and the ground began to shake.

"Earthquake!" one of the dads shouted.

Ant backed away from the house. A crack appeared in the grass, rapidly lengthening, snaking its way all around the main structure in a zigzagging circle but passing under the deck and then the garage. He watched, amazed, as the ground within that circle began to sink, taking the house with it, along with plant beds, bushes, part of the concrete path outside the front door, and the steps. Some of the deck descended too, but the rest stayed behind, cracking and splintering as it broke up.

He fell to his knees. Dimly aware of shouts and screams behind him, he remained where he was about twenty feet from the newly formed abyss into which the house was sinking. The modest property was gone in seconds, the roof vanishing from sight and leaving a shaft some fifty or sixty feet wide, its edges crumbling and cracking. Only the garage remained, along with the Mackenzies' cars in the driveway.

The grinding, crashing, booming noises continued for another half-minute, gradually receding while the shouts and screams behind him grew louder. Parents rushed past him to the edge of the abyss and threw themselves down on hands and knees to peer over the edge.

"Get back, get back!" Mr. Parker cried, yanking at his wife's feet as clods of turf tumbled away beneath her.

They all scrambled backward as sections of the shaft wall slid away and the rim widened. The twisted remainder of the deck teetered on the edge, secured by several concreted support posts that stuck firm. Dust plumed in the air, rolling outward across the lawn.

"Liam!" the Mackenzies screamed over and over.

"Madison!" her parents shouted.

A firm grip on Ant's shoulder caused him to wake from his shocked paralysis. He looked up to see Barton leaning over him. "Is this what you saw?" he whispered.

Looking again, Ant realized it was true. This was

exactly what he'd seen when he'd used the echo wand. From his limited vantage point in the lane, he'd assumed the hole in the ground was a burnt-out crater, but a closer inspection would have revealed to him this enormous, seemingly bottomless pit instead. The future really was set in stone, just open to interpretation.

"They're okay," he said softly. "Liam has seen himself as an old man. He's definitely okay."

"And Madison?"

"I . . . I don't know. I think so. The message she wrote to herself said I should stay away, but it didn't mention her or Liam because . . . because they were *meant* to be inside the house."

"*Meant* to be?" Barton repeated, sounding almost cross.

Ant climbed shakily to his feet. "I think that if I'd been inside, I probably would have died. Or might have. But Liam and Madison were never in danger. Maybe they got banged up a bit, but they're okay. I'm sure of it."

The more he spoke, the more he felt sure of their safety . . . even though his logic about Madison might be badly skewed.

He heard crying and turned to find Madison's little brother Cody standing alone, sobbing. Ant hurried over to comfort him, knowing the boy's parents were far too busy yelling for their lost daughter. "It's okay, buddy," he said over and over. "Kind of scary, right? But Liam and Madison are okay. They'll be back soon."

I hope.

Chapter 4

Liam stepped through the open doorway and out onto the deck, his rubber soles squeaking and flashlight beam quivering. There wasn't much of a deck left—just a few support beams nailed to the wall and a section of short, snapped-off decking planks. The rest was gone. It had been a good-sized area surrounded by fencing, decorated with pot plants, and furnished with a round glass table and four chairs, with a set of steps leading to the neatly cropped lawn. Now there was just a three-foot wooden ledge jammed up against a wall of solid rock.

"No way," he mumbled.

He remembered the scene outside his parents' bedroom window when the earthquake had started: the cars rising and the wall of rock moving up past the window. At the time, Liam had assumed the driveway had bulged upward, or perhaps he'd *wanted* to believe that, because the alternative was that the house had sunk into the ground. The thought had been nagging him since he'd crawled out of the closet and seen total darkness outside, and now he had to accept it as reality.

Ant's vision had come true, but not in the way he'd expected. The house hadn't been pulverized by an alien laser ray or meteor. It had sunk into the ground.

But where was the daylight above? The house's roof overhung, but there was still a big gap between the gutter and the rock wall. Even if it were the dead of night, wouldn't he see a glimmer of light up there somewhere? A faint glow of moonlight around the eaves? Flashlights pointing down at him? Why was nobody yelling his name?

All he could see was the rock wall all around. He had to get a better look.

With the flashlight gripped between his teeth, he found plenty of footholds in the twisted, broken siding. The house was only one story, and he knew he could make it onto the roof. When he reached the overhanging roof, the gutter cut into his hand as he pulled himself up and over. Moments later, he clambered onto the gritty tiled roof.

"Maddy?" he called. "You up here?"

The roof was badly warped but in one piece as far as he could see. It had only been repaired last weekend, and the contractors should be proud how well it had held up. He walked to its apex and stood there shining his flashlight around, a sense of utter doom descending on him.

The house was stuck at the bottom of a circular shaft only a fraction wider than the four corners of the house. The flashlight wasn't powerful enough to illuminate the walls higher up. He saw nothing but blackness, heard nothing but silence.

"HELLO!" he yelled at the top of his voice.

Only his echo replied.

He couldn't believe his house had fallen such a long way and not been smashed to bits. He thought back to the falling sensation followed by the deafening impact and bone-jarring scrapes. This was no earthquake. This was a *sinkhole*. He imagined the ground below the house had dropped away at a rapid but controlled speed, acting like a speeding elevator. The house had been supported the whole way down until it finally hit bottom.

Where had all the millions of tons of debris gone?

And more to the point, where was Madison? Her absence mystified him more and more.

"Madison!" he yelled, his voice echoing.

There had been many incidents of sinkholes on the news in recent years, mostly in Florida, but never on this scale. The shaft seemed endless, and *if* there was light at the top, then it was a mere pinprick. He squinted. Was he imagining that light?

Terror gripped him. How could he possibly be this deep underground? Just how long had he experienced the sensation of falling? It had seemed like just a few seconds, and yet here he was, seemingly miles underground. The foundations of the house and everything below it had literally run away like mud in a pipe, leaving an almost perfectly circular shaft.

Impossible, he thought.

He sat heavily, trembling all over. "I'm alive," he said aloud, liking the sound of his voice. Yes, he was alive. But how? He knew precious little about sinkholes but enough to know they were often deadly for families trapped inside homes. And surely this was the deepest sinkhole ever! He'd seen pictures of men rappelling into sinkholes, but usually only two or three hundred feet. Yet *this* one . . .

Liam peered up the shaft, finding it impossible to judge its distance but knowing it had to be hundreds, maybe even thousands of feet high. There was no sign of rescue workers, and Madison definitely hadn't climbed up on her own.

His parents had to be frantic by now. Madison's, too.

And Ant! Heck, even Barton must have raised a concerned eyebrow at the situation.

He remembered someone outside yelling his name as the tremors had started, probably his dad, and he hoped everyone had scrambled to safety before the ground gave way. They were probably up there now, shouting at firefighters and other emergency services to hurry up. *My son's down there*, Liam imagined his dad yelling. His mom was probably a puddle of tears.

As he stood there pondering, it occurred to him how warm it was. Shouldn't it be cool down here in the depths? *Unless we're near the Earth's core*, he thought with a shudder.

Shaking his head, he told himself to stop being so melodramatic. Still, he seemed to remember reading somewhere that tunnels and shafts were indeed warmer deep underground, but it was only noticeable at significant depths.

Looking up again, he thought, *This is pretty significant.*

He walked along the edge of the roof, turning at the corners until he was back where he'd started. The house was amazingly intact considering how far it had fallen. Even the landscaping around the building had survived to some degree, with a patch of grass here, part of a concrete path there, a flower bed, even part of the deck. A rectangular building filling a circular shaft—or a square peg in a round hole. *And no way out except up.*

He wished Madison would emerge from the darkness and call to him so they could be together again, safe and sound and sharing their misery. The reality was that he needed to head back down to the house to find her.

He jumped down, re-entered through the front door, and headed into the living room. The floor had a jagged crack across the middle. One wall bulged inward. Because the entire room was tilted, the sofa, armchairs, TV, coffee table, and numerous smaller furnishings had collected down the far end. Comically, a picture frame on the wall hung almost perfectly level as if stubbornly denying that a disaster had taken place.

The battery-powered clock on the wall told him it was just past eight-thirty. The disaster had occurred at 6:52. Taking into account perhaps half an hour of fumbled exploration, that meant he'd been unconscious for an hour or more. He tried to imagine Madison looking for him, calling out to him and receiving no answer, maybe using her phone to light her way. Had she come across his still body in the closet? If she had, she might have panicked and gone to get help. Or it could be she hadn't found him at all.

Or she might be lying somewhere, out cold, in much worse shape than him. That had to be it. He'd already been to the roof. There was literally no way out of this place, so she had to be in the house somewhere.

Liam headed for the hallway. He shone his flashlight into every ominous corner before proceeding. He wasn't normally afraid of the dark, but this was a suffocating blackness where all manner of underworld ghouls could be lurking.

"Maddy?" he called.

No answer.

He shuddered and navigated his way across the small lobby into the kitchen. He cracked open several drawers and cupboards, rummaging through the mess until he found five stubby candles and a box of matches. The first candle sputtered feebly, then flared. The yellow glow was welcoming, and Liam quickly lit the other four candles before the match burnt out. He slipped the flashlight and box of matches into his pocket.

With the candles alight, the kitchen immediately felt more homely. *No worse than a power outage*, he told himself. He continued to tell himself that as he picked up a couple of flickering candles and headed into the downward-sloping hall.

"Maddy!" he yelled for the umpteenth time. "Wake up! Where *are* you?"

Still nothing. Her silence worried him. She had to have been hit pretty hard on the head to be so out of it.

He braved a look into his bedroom, the glow of his candles sending pools of light across the buckled ceiling. The room was in terrible disarray, his computer and desk turned over onto the floor and buried in bits of drywall and layers of dust, his bookshelf and books somewhere among the debris. He stared sadly for a while, then crawled about the room looking in every place large enough to hide a frightened fourteen-year-old girl.

Nothing.

Growing puzzled, he glanced into the creepy laundry room next, holding aloft his two candles. He'd never liked its unfinished walls. The room seemed to be in a perpetual state of remodeling. His parents had been meaning to switch it around to make better use of the cramped space, maybe even doing a spot of decorating . . . but only his mom used the room, and it never seemed to be a matter of urgency. Now the washer and dryer had slid to the middle of the room, straining on their power cords and hoses.

But still no Madison. Not behind or between the appliances, nor in the narrow closet. He stared at the square hole in the floor, wondering if perhaps she'd fallen into it . . .

The bathroom was next. The toilet was intact even though the tank had cracked and leaked water everywhere. Not that it mattered. Figuring out where to pee was the least of his worries right now.

Madison wasn't here.

She had to be in the master bedroom. She'd been standing right there in the doorway when the house had sunk into the ground, and she must have fallen deeper into the room rather than try to dash away up the corridor. He must have crawled right past her earlier.

How lucky he'd been! This entire corner of the house had buckled so badly that the ceiling and walls practically lay across his bed. The closet he'd hidden in looked about the size of a shoebox, almost squashed flat.

"Maddy?" he said, softly again now. "Are you in here?"

Putting one candle down, he crawled on his knees with the other flickering flame held in front of him as he peered around and under the bed. She wasn't here. He checked the closet too.

Nothing.

No sign of her anywhere.

Chapter 5

Completely flummoxed by Madison's disappearance, Liam stood in his parents' destroyed bedroom trying to decide what to do next. He remembered the colorful glow sticks and dug around for them, knowing they'd spilled onto the floor. He stuffed as many as he could in his pockets.

He backed out of the bedroom, disappointed and bewildered. In the hall, he placed one of his candles on the floor in case he needed to return for some reason, then made his way back up the slippery floorboards toward the kitchen and living room.

Trying not to dwell on his failed exploration, he made himself busy depositing all the candles and glow sticks around the kitchen and living room. The sticks were different colors, so the effect was weird—sickly green by the small window, cool blue in the corner where the sofa had ended up, and creepy red along the wall backing onto the kitchen.

Could Madison have escaped the house before it sank into the ground? He didn't think so, yet she clearly wasn't here. It didn't make sense.

His thoughts drifted once more to the surface. What was everyone doing up there at this moment? In his mind he saw dozens of fire trucks, police cars, ambulances, crowds of people standing behind yellow tape that was stretched across the yard, his dad running around tearing his hair out, his mom and little sister clinging to each other and crying buckets ... and, in the middle of it all, reporters and TV cameras.

He hoped nobody else had been caught up in this. The idea of his parents or Ant lying buried in rubble somewhere filled him with horror. He shut out the thought and imagined himself as the sole victim in all this. Well, him and Madison, wherever she was.

The more he thought about the sinkhole, the more it didn't seem real. How could it be so deep? Where had all the displaced rock and earth gone? And why had the ground given way at all? They'd lived in the same house for years without any hint of drainage problems, one of the main causes for sinkholes.

Did Barton know something about this? The chauffeur had lived here himself once upon a time. Perhaps he knew of a network of tunnels deep below ground . . .

At that moment, he heard a shuffling noise. He listened, holding his breath.

The shuffling noise came again. He whipped the flashlight around. Was it in the room with him? No, it was in the hallway. Rescue workers? Doubtful. Rescue workers would be making a lot more noise, shining bright lights around and yelling his name. He'd likely have heard them stamping about on the roof.

So . . . what then?

He paused, listening hard. When the sound came again, Liam decided it definitely wasn't the scrabbling of a small rodent. It was bigger than that. It sounded like the shuffling of feet on a floor strewn with debris.

Madison!

He breathed a sigh of relief. "Hey, I'm in here," he called, getting to his feet. "Where have you been?"

He received no answer, but he heard a hasty scrambling as though someone were dashing away from his voice.

Liam hurried into the hallway, flashing his beam around but seeing nothing. "Maddy?" he called again, looking down the hallway. "Where are you?"

No answer.

Liam peered into each room as he went, shining his flashlight into every corner. First the kitchen, then his bedroom, then the laundry room—

He stopped and sniffed sharply. There was something nasty in the air. Not a skunk, but something just as pungent. It reminded him of a rotten onion his mom had discovered at the back of the cupboard one day. It had been *rank*.

Steeling himself, he flashed his light through the laundry room's doorway—and froze. Caught in the beam like a frightened deer, a man threw up his hands to shield against the glare. Liam glimpsed a ghastly face with bulbous staring eyes, the lipless teeth of a skull, tufts of hair sticking up from his bald head, small lumpy ears, oozing flesh . . .

Liam yelled and stumbled backward in horror. At the same time, the man dropped through the square hole in the floor, gone in an instant. Liam shook violently, his beam jerking across the room.

It was a while before he was able to force himself to move. Dropping to hands and knees, he scrambled across the floor and peered down into the hole. Roughly square, it looked like someone had smashed a way through the old subfloor. The floorboards on top, laid by his dad years ago, had broken apart with the all the twisting and buckling, revealing what seemed like an old, secret basement entrance. Except the house had no basement.

Nevertheless, his beam shone down past the broken ends of joists, blocks of concrete, and clumps of earth to a smooth, rock floor fifteen feet below.

"What the heck?" he muttered.

A makeshift rope of laundry hung from a joist. He recognized various garments belonging to him and his parents. They'd been tied together and used to climb down.

Madison?

What puzzled him was the faint yellow light emanating from the chamber, something he hadn't noticed earlier. Perhaps he would have if he'd peered into the laundry room in absolute darkness instead of shining his flashlight around. In any case, could this be a hidden room he never knew existed? Surely not. It had to be the bottom of the shaft. For some reason, the house hadn't quite plunged the entire way as he'd assumed. It had stopped short.

That didn't make sense either.

Maybe it was an existing tunnel, much narrower than the shaft itself. That seemed way too coincidental, though. And how had Madison known to cut a square hole in the laundry room floor? She couldn't have done that herself even if she'd had an inkling of a tunnel below.

But what other explanation was there? He studied the tunnel in the light of his flashlight, noting its sloping floor. He switched off his flashlight and studied it some more in its own faint glow. Maybe all the tons of rock and debris from the sinkhole had run off down this tunnel like muddy water in a pipe. Perhaps it was an old mine.

Puzzled but suddenly excited, Liam swung his legs over the side of the hole and prepared to jump down. Then he paused. A flash-image of the hideous man played over and over in his mind, a man whose face had partially melted away. He'd worn ragged, filthy clothes splashed with yellow stains. But no blood.

Liam shuddered.

Was the man someone he knew? His or Madison's dad? Barton? Thoughts of lava and boiling underground springs came to mind. He couldn't imagine anyone surviving a dunk in molten lava, but perhaps a scalding, bubbling pool . . . ? Why run away, though?

He shook his head. The man wasn't anyone he knew. He wasn't anyone from the surface. The man had been down here already, lurking in the tunnels, some kind of mutant. He *lived* down here, always scavenging for food.

Fear struck him. What if that . . . that *thing* had grabbed Madison?

It was a while before Liam felt safe to move. What if it got over its fright and came back? What if it was looking for food? What if it lived on raw meat and saw Liam as dinner?

He moaned quietly, his eyes squeezed shut. It was bad enough being trapped a hundred miles underground, but trapped with a flesh-eating monster with no face? It was too much. It wasn't fair!

Get a grip, he told himself. *Go find Maddy.*

But what if he ran across that lurking creature? Where had it come from exactly? Assuming it lived down here in the darkness, it had to have a place it called home. Maybe there were more of these creatures. The tunnel could be teeming with them. Maybe the tunnel led to a massive underground cavern. It would explain where all the tons of rock and dirt from the shaft had gone.

A few hours ago, Liam would have scoffed at all this even after his travels through wormholes to other planets. Now he believed anything was possible. Somewhere down there in the darkness, that half-melted faceless creature was shambling around chewing heads off rodents, a nightmarish monster living deep below the ground.

And now it might have Madison. He knew she was alive because he'd seen her in the future. He knew she hadn't had a leg chewed off or anything gruesome like that. But she still might be a prisoner somewhere, probably as scared as he was.

He had to go find her.

Chapter 6

Lurkers.

That was the name Liam gave to the hideous creatures who lived in the tunnels below the ground. His highly active imagination assured him there were more than one, probably dozens, and they ran around chewing on bugs and snakes and rodents and whatever else ran across their path.

With his flashlight in his pocket, he lowered himself down Madison's makeshift laundry rope with only the faint yellow light of the tunnel to see by. As he descended, ancient wall-mounted gas lamps came into view, with tiny flames that flickered in a breeze.

A breeze? That suggested this tunnel—about ten feet square—had an opening at both ends. The breeze headed downward.

Liam looked in both directions. Logic told him Madison should have headed uphill, only it was pitch-black that way. The soft light from the gas lamps led downhill only, starting at this exact point under the sinkhole shaft. There were no dormant gas lamps leading uphill. Another coincidence? It didn't make sense.

He turned this way and that, undecided. Uphill or down? Into darkness higher up—or follow the light down? Go against the breeze or with it? The air had to come from outside, right? But where was it going? Why would there be working gas lamps heading deep underground? And why start right here under the sinkhole shaft?

He decided the shaft had always been there. It must have been a way down to the mine. His house had been built precisely over the shaft on a thin layer of rock and earth.

No way, he thought.

Which way would Madison have gone? She was older than him, probably wiser, certainly more sensible. Whatever this place was, it stood to reason that the way out was up the tunnel into darkness. Even without a flashlight or candle, she could have used the light from her phone to guide the way. Or she might have taken a gas lamp from one of the walls.

A quick check told him that wasn't the case. None were missing that he could see.

He froze. Though the tunnel floor was smooth rock, the downhill slope was covered with a layer of loose soil and rubble—and what looked like fresh footprints. He thought one set could be Madison's, but another set had him worried, scuffed and haphazard as they were. The Lurker's?

Madison's prints led down the slope. Well, so be it. If she'd gone that way, then Liam would too.

* * *

A secret base, he suddenly thought after what seemed like hours of walking. *A military bunker, or a top-secret alien research center, like an underground version of Area 51.*

His heart began to hammer with excitement. This changed everything. If there were people down here, scientists and soldiers, then he and Madison were safe. Maybe there was a super-fast elevator to the surface.

It was a much more interesting theory than an abandoned mine. And anyway, what was the point of a ten-foot-wide tunnel stretching for miles underground but with no railroad tracks to cart the coal or other minerals out of the mine? A top-secret research base seemed more likely.

He walked faster, tripping on crumbling soil and piles of loose rock. He sank to his ankles with every step. The trek had gotten harder, and Madison's footprints were increasingly difficult to find. How far had he come? At three or four miles per hour, he must have traveled— what? Six miles or so? And all steadily downward. His feet ached, and he was drenched in sweat. The temperature seemed to be rising. Only the thought of finding Madison ahead kept him going.

Doubts still nagged at him. If a top-secret underground Government base lay ahead, then maybe the personnel wouldn't return him and Madison to the surface after all. Maybe they would quietly 'do away' with the intruders rather than reveal their location. He had to be sure, though. Just to know there were other people— *normal* people—underground with him would make him feel a whole lot better.

He wondered about the Lurker as he tramped along. Probably an escaped experiment, a genetic mutation of some kind. A horrible thought but probably to be expected with this kind of sinister operation. Liam would be wary. The creature might be perfectly harmless, a poor shuffling creature rejected and shunned by the evil scientists, left to forage in the darkness for food. And hopefully there was just one rather than dozens.

So many gas lamps, he thought again. Spaced twenty

feet apart and hanging on both sides of the tunnel, Liam had assumed there to be an automated mechanism to light them all, like a continuous gas feed and a simple sparker. Instead, each lamp was a simple flame, like that of a candle only without the candle! He didn't know exactly how they worked, but he knew nobody in their right mind would light them individually. Not this many. Madison certainly wouldn't have. Maybe one every so often, but not every twenty feet and on both sides of the tunnel.

Gandalf the wizard lit them. It's the only explanation. A magic wand or something.

He tripped on something hard, a large, random, twisted bit of metal, obviously from a substantial structure but certainly not part of the house. He found another piece moments later, sticking up out of the dirt, and then another soon after, although this piece was a thin, buckled sheet about his height. There could be many more buried pieces for all he knew, because the dirt was much deeper now.

His mind was so full of rambling thoughts of conspiracies and buried alien spaceships that it took him a while to notice a square of glowing white light ahead.

Relieved but also apprehensive, he broke into a jog. He saw bushes and ferns overhanging the end of the tunnel, moving gently in the breeze. It looked like daylight out there, but it couldn't be. Not real daylight, anyway. He'd been heading downhill the whole time, and besides, it wasn't morning yet. He'd walked for a long time, but not *that* long. It couldn't be past midnight.

Never mind that, he told himself. *I'm out!*

He squinted as he rushed down the last few yards. The glaring light made it impossible to see clearly. He tripped and crawled, his hands grasping clumps of soil, thick weeds and roots, and then he was out, warmth flooding over him as he emerged into blinding daylight.

Something weird happened. His stomach lurched, and the ground seemed to tilt under his feet. He stumbled and fell into the ferns.

Liam got up on his knees and shielded his eyes, blinking rapidly. At first he kept his gaze low, panning from side to side. *How can this be?* he wondered, seeing thick vegetation, lots of ugly bushes, a few trees here and there. *I'm outside! I'm back on the surface!*

As his eyes adjusted to the glare, he looked farther and spotted rooftops—ordinary houses, although rather quaint and old, made of stone with chimneys and slate roofs. Not exactly what he'd expected, but okay. He didn't recognize the neighborhood at all. Maybe Edensville? No, it was nothing like Edensville. It was nothing like anywhere he'd been before.

Why is it daytime? Did I lose time somewhere along the way?

He again felt a lurch of dizziness, a touch of vertigo, as his gaze moved higher. He was seeking the horizon, only there wasn't one. The countryside just kept on going, up and up, higher and higher, like the world had been inverted and he was inside a giant bowl whose inhabitants were clinging to the inner surface. No, not a bowl but a *sphere*, miles across, surrounding him. Liam gasped, seeing a tiny group of houses high above his head in the hazy distance, defying gravity, hanging upside down as the world curved around and around . . .

Then he fainted.

Chapter 7

Ant stayed well clear of the emergency services. Flashing blue lights lit up the trees, and the lawn was filled with fire trucks, police cars, an ambulance, and a few other people called in because of their so-called expertise in such things as sinkholes.

The Mackenzies and the Parkers, along with little Cody, had been ushered next door to Madison's house to sit out the rescue and keep out of the way. But the two dads couldn't be still, and they'd stomped back out to the disaster zone and split up to independently demand action.

It had been an unbearable four or five hours since the event, and Ant hadn't seen much progress. Seeing the incident live on the 11 PM local news, his own parents called and ordered him to come home and explain what was happening, and he did so with great reluctance . . . and then returned to the disaster zone afterward, prepared to wait out the rescue no matter how long it took.

There was barely room to steer the limousine past the crowd and parked vehicles in the lane. When Ant stepped out and pushed through the crowd to the yellow CAUTION tape, he had a sudden moment of *déjà vu* and paused with a jolt of shock. He felt a prickly sensation on the back of his neck and stood perfectly still, knowing he was being watched—by a future version of himself!

He remembered the moment well. He'd used the echo wand to visit the future, and he'd seen *this*—himself stepping out of the limo and approaching the yellow tape to gaze with amazement at the massive hole in the ground where Liam's house had once stood. From here it actually did look like a laser bolt from space had incinerated it, absolutely nothing left but a hole in the ground.

He felt the presence lift and risked a glance behind. He saw nothing untoward, but others in the crowd seemed perturbed, glancing around as if they'd gotten a chill down their spine.

At first, the police didn't let him pass under the CAUTION tape. But when Barton stepped up behind him, they recognized him from earlier and allowed the two of them through. Ant found that annoying. So it was okay for a 'responsible adult' to re-enter but not a kid? He tried not to scowl at the officers as he passed them.

Ant sought out Liam's dad and hung close, overhearing conversations with one of the experts. "Why aren't you lowering people down on ropes?" Mr. Mackenzie demanded.

"Because we need to set up a hoist," the gnarly, unshaven man said patiently. "The top of the shaft is undercut in places, so we can't just lower ropes over the unstable edge, because even the weight of a rescue worker will cause the rope to cut into the rim and dislodge more rock and dirt, and that could be dangerous for anyone below. Plus the severed water pipe drenched the walls of the shaft, making it soft and wet in places."

"So use a hoist!"

"We have a small, portable crank drum with us, but we need something bigger to span the gap. Also, it comes with a nine-hundred-foot rope, but we estimate this shaft to be much deeper."

"So when are you going in?"

"When the bigger hoist is here, and when we can ascertain that the—"

"Why not use a helicopter?" Liam's dad persisted, waving his arms about. "It's clear above. Lower someone down on a rope. Heck, lower *me* down on a rope."

"A helicopter, sir? This shaft is well over two thousand feet! That's about half a mile. It's four times the height of Ellison's Cave not far from here, the deepest known cave pit in the United States. This may be part of that cave system, but we're not sure. Or maybe it's an old mine; some of those run really deep, but usually not this wide, and anyway, there's no record of it. Look, I know it's hard to wait, but believe me, safety is paramount. If rescue workers are hurt on the way down, or we cause the shaft walls to collapse, then the situation could quickly escalate into something much, much worse—"

"So how long?"

The expert shrugged. "Rescue operations like this can take twenty-four hours, sometimes days. This shaft seems to be absolutely vertical, which will certainly speed things up. But it's also incredibly deep and wide. Once the equipment is here . . ."

Ant couldn't get over what the man had said about the shaft being half a mile deep. Who would even want to descend such a vast distance on a thin rope? How long would it take on a motorized winch?

He had faith in the rescue services, but it worried him how unnatural and extraordinary this shaft was. Whatever the explanation, it had drawn a lot of interest. More and more experts were being called in, and everyone seemed extremely cautious about how to proceed. This rescue wouldn't be over anytime soon, especially since it was already midnight and they were waiting on some more equipment.

Barton approached. "Let's go for a ride, Master Anthony."

"What? We just got here! I'm not going home again."

"No, not home. I want to find something. And I need to tell you about Caleb."

Caleb? His long-lost son? The one he hasn't seen in over twenty years?

Barton had mentioned the boy just last weekend, but he hadn't made a whole lot of sense. For one thing, he still thought Caleb was eight years old—not figuratively but literally. That didn't make any sense unless time travel was involved. Also, Barton had once lived in this same house with his wife and son long before Liam's family had come along, and he'd insisted on keeping a close eye on the house over the years, fearful his son would 'show up again' one day. The story was rather kooky at best.

Intrigued, Ant allowed himself to be led back to the limousine, much to the satisfaction of the police. Reporters pounced on them at once, looking for new information, but Barton warded them off and opened the door for Ant to climb inside—not the rear door as usual, but the front passenger door.

When they were safely cruising up the lane toward the highway, Ant looked sideways at his driver. "So where are we going?"

The man's expression gave nothing away. "It's a short drive, so let me start at the beginning and tell you as fast as I can. You'll find this very difficult to believe."

"Ha!" Ant scoffed. "I've seen quite a lot of incredible stuff lately. I doubt you'll surprise me."

"Well, we'll see."

Something in his voice set Ant's nerves on edge. He fell silent and waited while Barton collected his thoughts. They were already turning right on the highway by the time he began.

"My name used to be Hugh. Hugh Ratcliff. I was happily married to Rose until Caleb came along. Then things became . . . strained. He was just four when Rose left us. She couldn't bear it any longer. She loved him but was absolutely terrified of him. As far as she was concerned, he needed to be institutionalized. It wasn't that he was crazy, simply that he was a four-year-old wielding immense power. He could cause enormous damage just by thinking about it, and his short temper didn't help matters. I understood her concern, but I guess he was a daddy's boy and responded to me better. I managed him quite well most of the time.

"We had a dog once. That stupid mutt barked once too often, and Caleb thought it would be helpful if he sealed up the dog's mouth to keep him quiet. He did so, but he also sealed up the nostrils. I don't mean he used tape or anything mundane like that. I mean he made the mouth and nose vanish. They just weren't there anymore. Instead, the dog's muzzle was smooth and featureless, nothing but short hair, no openings at all. Needless to say, he died a minute later.

"Now, that doesn't mean Caleb was mean. He was just . . . young. He bawled his eyes out when he realized what he'd done, and he tried to recreate the dog, but it didn't work. The imitation *looked* the same, but it didn't *act* the same. It made some dog noises as you'd might expect, and it ate food and slept and wagged its tail, but it

44

was clearly not the same dog, nor any other dog. It lacked something. It had no soul. And it was repetitive, like it had been programmed to follow a basic routine. Nothing but a lifeless mechanical toy."

Ant already regretted scoffing at Barton's definition of 'difficult to believe.' He almost stopped him and proclaimed the driver's story as wacky, but he bit his tongue and held off. After all, Madison writing herself sleep messages was hard to believe. So were wormholes. And his best friend turning into a robot for a day was a doozy!

"So Rose left us. She couldn't take the stress anymore, and she knew I would never forgive her if she quietly turned Caleb over to the authorities so they could poke and prod at him. I believe to this day that a boy who can create things out of thin air would certainly be coerced into producing weapons. In fact, Caleb wouldn't *need* to create weapons. He could destroy an army just by thinking about it."

Barton gave Ant a sideways look and smiled before returning his gaze to the road.

"This was when Caleb was four," he went on. "That was twenty-seven years ago. Rose left, and I raised Caleb alone for the next four years. We lived in the very same house Liam lives in—or *did* live in before it fell into the ground. I couldn't work a job like most people simply because I couldn't leave Caleb alone with strangers. I homeschooled him and earned a living selling duplicates."

"Duplicates?" Ant repeated, feeling weak.

"He was able to create copies of objects. TVs, for instance. We had one in every room just because it suited him. Exact copies down to every last detail . . . except on the inside. Because what Caleb couldn't see didn't seem to matter. The outside of the TV was exquisitely perfect in every way, but the inside was blank. I opened one up and found nothing but a hazy blackness. It was unfinished, yet it worked perfectly. If Caleb wanted it to work, it simply worked, with or without electricity. It didn't even need a satellite dish or receiver. He expected cartoons to play, and play they did.

"So I sold TVs on a regular basis, fetching a few hundred dollars for each. I had quite a few contacts who never asked questions." He looked a little sheepish at this, and he sighed. "I told you I wasn't a good man."

Right, Ant thought. *You got my previous driver fired by stashing alcohol in the trunk of the limo, and then you stepped in and took his job. And all because I'm Liam's best friend and you wanted to keep an eye on his house.*

Ant said nothing, though. As far as he was concerned, his driver had a mysterious past but was at heart a good person.

"I guess selling duplicates conjured from thin air wasn't exactly stealing," Barton said. "Not in the traditional sense, anyway. I sold all kinds of things. I once took Caleb to a jewelry store and let him hold an actual diamond. It was a very risky day out, but well worth it. After that, Caleb could make his own diamonds— absolutely perfect replicas. I sold one or two."

Ant would have imagined duplicated diamonds to be a fast-track solution to immense wealth. "Why just a couple?"

"They attracted too much attention. TVs were safer. I made enough money to survive comfortably while staying under the radar. However, the IRS caught up with me by the time Caleb was eight. I avoided the audits, and we had to disappear in a hurry when the police eventually came knocking."

Barton took a left turn along a twisty lane. Ant had been out this way once or twice. It had to be nearly ten miles of countryside before hitting the outskirts of Edensville, an even sleepier town than Brockridge. Where were they headed?

"You disappeared?" Ant pressed. He'd gleaned this much from a previous conversation with his driver. "Where to?"

With a faint smile of remembrance, Barton sighed and said, "We went underground."

Chapter 8

When his head stopped spinning, Liam opened his eyes. Then wished he hadn't.

Far above, where the sky should be, he saw forests and hills hanging upside down, stretching in all directions, wrapping around the inside of a colossal sphere several miles across. It made him dizzy to look, yet he was scared not to. When he craned his neck and stared directly upward, he felt as though he were in freefall, plummeting to his death. Yet he felt the reassuring ground under his knees and groping hands.

He shielded his eyes against the glare of the sun, then realized it couldn't possibly be the sun and spent the next minute trying to figure out what the blinding light was. It hung at a point dead center of the sphere and *appeared* to be about the size of the sun, and just as dazzling. And hot, too; he felt its rays on his skin and saw the shadows it cast on the soil beneath him. The ball of fire looked like the sun, only it *wasn't* the sun. It couldn't be. The real sun was over a hundred times bigger than the Earth and about ninety million miles distant. This ball of fire couldn't be much more than a mile away and had no business floating in midair like that. It was big and hot, and incredibly bright, but not a *sun*. Not a real one.

Liam found himself breathing hard and dripping with sweat, yet his hands were icy cold. He remained in the dirt surrounded by bushes, afraid to move. A constant breeze moved the leaves and ruffled his hair. The breeze was cool and strong and came from the tunnel he'd stumbled out of. The entrance to the tunnel was dark and ominous, a ten-foot-square shaft leading straight down even though he'd just walked along it and stepped out. Nothing made sense, but right now Liam needed to keep it within his sight.

Tons of dirt and rock had recently spilled from the tunnel and scattered across the immediate area. *The contents of the shaft*, he thought. Even so, it didn't seem realistic somehow. It was what he called 'movie logic'—a detail added for realism but with only a token effort made by the set designers, not fully researched or given the attention it deserved. It was fake-looking.

Buried in the dirt were two twisted bicycles, one larger than the other. They seemed completely out of place. Unable to fathom their significance, he dismissed them from his already confused mind.

He focused instead on the nearby village with its stone-walled houses and slate-tile roofs. It looked like something from the TV, a quaint little English place with cobbled roads and stone walls. A small village, hardly more than a main street with a couple of alleys leading off. There was no sign of life. Beyond the village, endless fields began the gradual climb up the inside of the sphere, continuing up and up. Liam again felt his gaze drawn to the miniature sun and hurriedly returned his attention to the village.

The main road angled out past the houses on the far side and cut through the fields. Liam followed its long, winding path up and around the sphere, and once again had to shield his eyes against the sun as his gaze reached the halfway point directly opposite. He skipped past the glare and picked up the road again as it meandered onward, finally heading back down the curve on the other side. He saw that it came within a hundred feet of where he was sitting, then arrived back at the village and rejoined itself. A single, continuous road that literally circled the world.

Everything was rolling green hills or expanses of forest, almost green overkill. Where was the ocean? Liam saw a few narrow rivers and a small lake . . . but no ocean. And no sky, although there were fluffy white clouds here and there, hanging low and drifting lazily.

He rubbed his eyes for the umpteenth time. He was never going to get used to this. Every time he thought he had it straight, his gaze would drift upward and he'd be overcome with dizziness. *Humans aren't supposed to see this*, he thought suddenly. *We walk around the outside of the world, not the inside. This can't be happening. This isn't real.*

A small, logical voice in his head reminded him that this strange inner world was nowhere near the size of Earth. It wasn't like the planet was completely hollow and the Government had somehow found a way to build on the inside. Earth was nearly eight thousand miles in diameter whereas this strange place spanned a few miles at most, nothing but a tiny air bubble just below the Earth's surface. *An air bubble*, Liam thought dreamily. *Yes, that's it. A naturally formed bubble caused by molten plasma that . . . that . . .*

He gave up. Nothing could explain this place. The miniature sun, the gravity, the pretty landscape, even the quaint English village—none of it made sense.

Liam climbed to his feet, swayed, and nearly fell over again. He stumbled to the nearest tree and leaned against it. Its branches partially blocked the glare of the sun above and allowed him to get a better look around without the need to squint.

Some of the hills were shaped like mountains but relatively small. One in particular stood higher than the rest and was open-topped like a volcano. It was located high and to his left, jutting directly toward the sun like a massive cannon. For a moment, Liam had the crazy idea that the volcano had just shot forth a ball of fire and everything was frozen in time. But of course it would seem that way; just about anything that stood upright in this impossible inside-out world would look like it was reaching for the sun at its center.

Liam tried in vain to stop looking upward, but every time he glanced around he found his gaze drawn higher. There was no horizon, no natural boundary between land and sky. The hills kept on going up and around, and so did his gaze.

"Focus," he muttered, clutching his face to forcibly prevent himself from craning his neck. He looked toward the village again. Thin trails of smoke rose from several chimneys. "So there's life, then," he said aloud, reassured by the sound of his own voice.

The idea of a secret Government base was slipping away. If the Government possessed the technology and the means to build a place like this, surely they wouldn't build a sleepy English village in the middle of lush green countryside. The place would probably be endless desert and military buildings swarming with soldiers. Jeeps and Hummers mounted with machine guns would be speeding around. It would be a hive of activity, with secret hangars surrounded by electrified fences . . .

Liam shook his head. He really didn't know *what* a secret Government base would look like. He just knew it wouldn't include quaint stone cottages.

He turned and stared at the tunnel. *His* tunnel. It was still there, an open black pit partially obscured by ferns that were moving in the breeze. The square tunnel was his only way out of this madness, and he didn't want to lose sight of it. If he strayed too far, he might never find his way back.

On the other hand, he couldn't stand around forever. He had to find help. And he had to find Madison.

He studied the scenery around the tunnel, noting several natural landmarks that he could pick out from a distance: three trees standing in a triangle here, a blackened stump over there, and the tunnel about halfway between. And the tons of scattered dirt and rock looked like a brown stain on the green landscape.

With a sigh of trepidation, Liam set off.

Chapter 9

It wasn't far to the village. Liam kept expecting a U.S. Army Hummer to come tearing around a corner, but all was quiet. The High Street was narrow and paved with dashed white lines painted down the center. Sidewalks lined both sides, and old-fashioned shiny black lampposts perfectly suited the Victorian shop fronts. If it were snowing, it would be a great setting for a Charles Dickens movie.

Modern storefront goods and illuminated signs over the windows reassured Liam that he hadn't stepped back in time. He stopped to peer into the nearest boutique, which offered a delicious array of truffles and chocolates. The sign read *Harlequin Delights* in swirling letters, and the chocolate aroma wafting out of the door was enough to make Liam drool. If he was going to ask for help, this would be as good a place as any.

He pushed the door open, and a little bell rang above his head as he stepped inside the small shop. The smell of chocolate almost overpowered him. There were truffles of all flavors, many with multicolored sprinkles and white powder coating. They filled the wood-framed cabinet walls as well as the glass counter he stood before.

Liam waited for someone to appear, then re-opened the shop door to make the bell ring again, stamping his feet noisily as though just entering. He closed the door with a bang and waited a little longer.

"Hello?" he called at last.

Behind the counter, an open door led to a dark corridor. He assumed the shop owner was visiting the restroom or making a cup of coffee—or more likely hot tea if this place was modeled on an English village. Liam was sure someone would be along in a moment.

A full minute ticked by, and Liam grew impatient. He stepped around the counter and peered past the door to the hallway beyond. He saw no sign of movement, nor even a glimmer of light. Perhaps the owner was out. Still, there had to be a phone somewhere. Liam didn't see one behind the counter, so he took a few steps into the dark hallway, absently feeling in his pocket for his flashlight.

Something was wrong. It was too quiet, too dark. Liam strained to see ahead but found only blackness. He couldn't locate a light switch, so he pulled out his flashlight and switched it on. The beam lit up the walls and floor to his sides but somehow petered out a few feet ahead. Liam took a few steps, his free hand groping.

As he edged forward, his fingers faded into nothingness, then his hand and his wrist. He gasped and jerked back. There was something *very* wrong here. Just for a moment he had felt a curious smothering sensation in the hall ahead. He flashed his beam directly in front of him, but the darkness swallowed up the light.

Liam backed up and returned to the shop. The novelty of the cozy, quaint English boutique deserted him. Now he just felt a need to leave. Even the smell of chocolate was making him feel sick. He dashed outside.

"It's the Twilight Zone," he muttered. "Everybody's disappeared. The town is made of paper mache."

The next shop was crammed with hand-woven baskets and cloth bags with flowery designs embroidered on the sides. All very cute, but the place appeared to be devoid of life and therefore no interest whatsoever to Liam. He moved on.

Shop after shop, he saw no sign of anyone. He risked a quick visit inside a dusty secondhand bookshop and, completely alone, peered around a number of precarious shelving racks with an array of bizarre titles like *Book About Towns* and *Lots of Small Writing*. He moved on to the next shop, a mobile phone store, extremely bare and boring. Again he moved on. He resisted the temptation to enter a bakery named *Buns In The Oven* even though it smelled great. Pastries lined the window, brown and unusually shiny, steaming as if pulled from the oven moments before. They were called Cornish Pasties. Liam had no idea what was inside them, but the smell made his stomach rumble. The bread rolls, too, looked amazing—

He shook himself. He couldn't stand around gawking at food. He had to find a phone. It was true that he had just passed a mobile phone shop, but he knew none of the devices on display would actually be connected and usable. He needed a normal, working landline and a person to talk to.

Liam crossed the street, thinking he had seen movement. He was drawn to a place called *Ming's*, which he guessed was a Chinese takeaway. Yet the smell wafting out the open door wasn't Chinese food; it smelled more like fish.

"Fish and chips!" he exclaimed. Of course. This place was modeled on an English village, after all.

He froze in the middle of the street as he saw movement again. Yes, someone was in *Ming's*—a woman with short black hair, wearing a black shirt and a white apron. She was moving to and fro, wielding a long pair of tongs and leaning over the tall aluminum counters.

Liam burst inside and confronted her. "Can you help me?"

The woman looked up and smiled sweetly. She was Asian, possibly Chinese although Liam was no expert. Was Ming a Chinese name? He really had no clue. "What you like?" she said in broken English.

"I need a phone," Liam said. "I need to—"

"Portion of chips?" she interrupted, still smiling. She gestured into the counter. The top was glass, and Liam glanced down to see a mass of thick, steaming steak fries—or chips as the Brits called them. "Fish? Steak pie?" she urged.

Liam frowned. "What?"

"You want fish and chips, yes?"

"No, I need a phone. I need to call home." When the smile remained fixed on the woman's face, he added, "I need to call the police."

"Fish and chips? Steak pie?" the woman went on, beaming and nodding. "Battered sausage? Pickled onion?"

She gestured wildly at the array of bizarre foods. "No," he said firmly. "I need a phone. A *phone*." He put a fist to the side of his head and spread his thumb and pinkie. "See? I need to make a phone call."

"Cod or haddock?"

"I don't want any food!" he yelled.

The woman's smile faltered. Immediately Liam felt sorry.

"Look, I just need help. I don't know where I am. My house fell into a sinkhole, and I ended up here. Can you tell me where this is? This village? Where are we?"

The woman looked confused and forlorn.

Liam tried again. "A phone. Do you have a phone? A telephone?"

The woman seemed to have slipped into a trance. She stared past him out the window, then lifted the tongs and studied them with a frown. As if Liam wasn't there, she reached down and began moving large battered fillets of fish around, organizing them.

Liam stared at her, his heart sinking into his stomach. Something was definitely wrong.

Chapter 10

Liam abandoned the fish-and-chip shop. The Chinese woman had started beaming again, asking if he wanted a portion of chips as if the previous conversation had been blotted from her memory. He hurried out, a feeling of desperation sweeping over him. Something had occurred to him, something horrible and terrifying.

What if he was dead?

Maybe he'd pushed the universe too far this time. Maybe he'd been sent to an alternate world. Or maybe this was The Afterlife.

It made sense. How could he have survived that sinkhole anyway? He was lying dead in the rubble somewhere and only *thought* he was still alive, and his ghostly spirit was walking around some kind of purgatory. That was why everything felt so weird.

Still, if he had retained all his faculties, why hadn't the Chinese woman? She was clearly off her rocker. Maybe she'd been in limbo too long and lost her mind.

He trudged along the road, walking on the painted white lines at its center. With the sun directly overhead, his shadow pooled around his feet. He assumed it always would no matter what time of day it was. Was there such a thing as night here?

He heard nothing but his own breaths and soft footfalls. Some might call this village peaceful and serene, but to Liam it was deathly silent—no birds chirping, no dogs barking, no cars revving. Even in the quietest neighborhood, the distant drone of cars could usually be heard. Here, there was nothing.

The High Street remained straight until the shops petered out, after which it curved sharply to the right and disappeared around the corner. Over the rooftops, the road reappeared in the distance as a thin gray line curving up the spherical landscape through fields and meadows. Liam squinted, seeing something rectangular to the side of the road among a clump of trees. Was that a car? Yes, it *was*. But it was stationary. He watched it as he walked, but it refused to move. Perhaps it had been abandoned.

He paused. He had left the shops behind and was now at an intersection. He peered to his left where a row of townhouses lined one side of a short road. A low stone wall bordered the other side, open fields beyond.

It occurred to Liam that perhaps the village was simply closed up for the day. It was Sunday morning after all.

His pulse quickened. He should go knock on some doors. *That* was where the villagers were—lounging in front of the TV or relaxing with a good book. Everybody was at home today, or maybe at a church somewhere.

He counted nine or ten sturdy front doors with brass knockers. "Here goes nothing," he muttered as he approached the first.

There was no lawn, just a single stone step right off the sidewalk. The red-painted door had a hefty brass knocker shaped like a lion's head. It all looked ordinary enough except for a horizontal, rectangular slot in the door, inside which a bundle of mail was jammed tight.

He rapped the knocker and stood back. The street remained silent.

The mail protruding from the slot suggested that the homeowner wasn't in. And there was an unpleasant smell, too. Liam leaned closer, sniffed, and recoiled. It smelled like rotting onions, just like—

He paused, frowning at the door. The smell from within was familiar, like the hideous man with the melted face he'd seen in his house. The Lurker.

Unsure what to make of this, Liam hurried away, his mind whirling. He skipped a couple of houses and rapped on the door of the fourth, noting that this one's mail slot was properly closed.

The door opened quickly as if the owner had been waiting for him. Liam almost jumped out of his skin in surprise. An old man peered down at him from his high doorstep. He wore brown pants and a dark red sweater, and he had a huge beak nose and shaggy grey eyebrows. "Not today, thanks," the man said dully.

He went to close the door again, but Liam leapt onto the doorstep and planted his hands on the door. "Wait—I need help. Can I use your phone?"

The old man frowned. "I don't want to buy anything," he insisted. His accent was strange. It *might* be British but had one of their many odd regional twangs.

"I'm not selling anything," Liam assured him. "I just need to borrow your phone. I need to call the police."

He thought that mentioning the police would speed things along, but the old man simply stood there shaking his head. "I'm not interested," he said firmly. "Whatever you're selling, I don't want it."

"I'm not selling anything!" Liam yelled, hopping up and down. "I just need a phone! What's *wrong* with you people?"

"Not today, thanks," the old man said. And he closed the door.

Liam was livid. He kicked the door savagely before he could stop himself. Then he hurried on to the next house.

Before he arrived, the door opened and a stern-faced woman stepped out with a basket slung across her arm. She pulled her door shut with a bang and started walking toward Liam. He stopped, hopeful.

She walked straight past him without giving him a glance.

"Excuse me," Liam said, hurrying after her. She walked fast. Her long skirt flapped around her legs, and her nylon stockings made a *thwip-thwip* sound in time with the clacking of her heels. "Hello? I need—uh, ma'am?"

She ignored him. When she reached the end house, she paid no attention to the nasty smell emanating from the jammed mail slot. She marched on and turned the corner.

Liam almost gave up but then ran after her in a sudden rage. He jumped in front of her, turned, and stopped dead. Either she would notice him or try to walk right through him.

A spark of puzzlement flickered across her face, and she faltered. Then she sidestepped around him and continued. But Liam caught her arm and gripped it tight, planting his feet firmly and refusing to be dragged along. He tried to ignore how cold her skin was.

She had no choice but to notice him. "Can't stop," she said firmly. "Got to get some shopping done before dinner."

"I need a phone," Liam said grimly.

"Can't stop," the woman repeated. "Got to get some shopping done before dinner."

She waited, neither tugging her arm free nor offering him eye contact. For a moment, the two of them were like statues, frozen in time. Then Liam released her. Without further delay, she clacked away on her heels, skirt swishing.

Liam peered with disgust at his fingers, which were coated with some kind of sticky substance. He sniffed them cautiously. "Onions! What the heck?"

As he looked around for something to wipe his fingers on, he spotted a big red telephone booth on the opposite side of the High Street. His jaw dropped open. He'd walked right past it earlier, apparently too busy staring at the impossible sun to notice what he'd been looking for all along.

The woman with the basket entered *Buns In The Oven*. As she disappeared inside, Liam glared at the back of her head and reached down to wipe his sticky fingers on the pavement. Then he hurried across the street and pulled open the door of the booth. It was surprisingly heavy. As it closed behind him, he wrinkled his nose at the smell. Not rotten onions but something entirely more familiar. "Someone's been using this as a restroom," he mumbled.

He picked up the clunky handset and put it to his ear. He heard nothing.

The stainless steel keypad had a slot for coins, but Liam's pockets were empty except for his flashlight and box of matches. Still, he was pretty sure he wouldn't need money to call the police. He dialed 9-1-1, jabbing the buttons viciously. It rang and rang, and Liam waited with increasing anxiety. The Brits used 9-9-9 for emergency services, but this was merely an imitation village. It was still America, after all.

Just when he thought it would never answer, a familiar girl's voice whispered, "Hello?"

Liam almost dropped the phone. "Maddy? Is that you?"

Chapter 11

Ant watched the trees rushing past his window as the limousine cruised along the winding lane. Barton's story was becoming more and more bizarre.

"The police pounded on the door. I always kept the house bolted in case the police, taxmen, or even criminals came sniffing around, so I had a few more minutes to spare. I told Caleb we needed to leave this place behind, that we needed to escape. I asked if he wanted to play a game. Well, of course he did. He treated it like cops and robbers." The hint of a smile crept across his face. "You see, Master Anthony, I always knew how to manipulate Caleb into doing things he wouldn't necessarily be interested in otherwise. I made things into games, and I praised him every chance I got."

He went on to explain how he'd taken Caleb into the laundry room and asked if he could make a hole in the floor, a tunnel to escape through. Caleb had been delighted, because it was something he'd never been allowed to do before.

"So he made a hole," Barton said. "The floorboards just came loose. I pulled them out of the way, which itself was remarkable since they were supposed to be tongue-and-groove fitted. They came up a little too easily. Underneath was a roughly square hole through the subfloor and foundation. It led down into an elevator car."

"What?" Ant exclaimed, unable to contain himself.

The man smiled. "Yes, I know, but bear with me, will

you? You see, Caleb told me he'd always wanted to be a miner. I think he'd watched a TV show a few days before. Anyway, he got the idea of an elevator leading straight down to a mine far, far underground. So as we stood there in the laundry room with the police banging on the door, he closed his eyes, and I heard that whispering sound—the same sound I always hear when he creates something— and suddenly there it was, an old mining elevator beneath our feet. He remembered all the details from the TV show he'd watched."

"Wait, hold on a minute," Ant said. "I don't buy it. He *remembered* how to build an elevator? All those working parts, all that detail? He just remembered it all?"

Barton tapped his fingers on the steering wheel as he picked up speed on a straight stretch of road. "You've heard of regression by hypnosis, yes?"

"Uh . . . sure."

"Let's say a witness to a murder can't remember anything useful about the crime. He could be put under hypnosis, and while in that relaxed state, he manages to recall details that had eluded him before. Tapping into the subconscious mind can be a very valuable tool. The conscious mind is a busy, bustling, noisy place, full of readily available information . . . but only the things you choose to remember, what you think of as the important stuff. How many stairs are in your house?"

The question threw Ant for a loop. "What?"

"It's a classic Sherlock Holmes question: How many stairs are in your house? Come on, now. Think about the flight of stairs to your bedroom. You walk up and down those at least twice every single day. You've lived in that house all your life. That's . . ."

Barton drummed his fingers again, his lips moving soundlessly as he worked it out.

In the end, he shrugged. "Well, it has to be at least six thousand times. Maybe ten thousand. Anyway, the point is, you go up and down every day, but you don't know how many steps there are. You *see*, but you don't *observe*."

"So?" Ant muttered.

"So, if you were put under hypnosis and asked to recall how many steps there are, I'll bet you could do it. Your subconscious mind is far more powerful than your conscious one. Every detail is stored there whether you know it or not. Everything you've ever seen and learned is right there. We just find it hard to access it."

"But Caleb can?" Ant guessed, seeing where Barton was going with this.

"I don't understand how, and nor does he, but he recreated that elevator perfectly—at least as far as the TV show permitted. He never saw the elevator motor system above, so he had no concept of how that worked or even that it existed. He created an elevator with fuzzy areas. It worked perfectly, but it really shouldn't have. It was literally below the floor of the laundry room, and we dropped down through its ceiling. There were no cables, not even a motor room. If I'd pointed out the flaws in his logic, the elevator wouldn't have worked."

Ant spent a long time digesting this, and he was glad Barton paused to let him. "Like a cartoon, then," he said finally.

"*Exactly* like that!" Barton exclaimed, and Ant looked at him in surprise. "Like Wile E. Coyote and the Roadrunner, his favorite show. The coyote would run off a cliff and only start falling when he realized there was no ground under his feet."

Oh boy, Ant thought. He was conflicted. He wanted to believe Barton, probably *did* believe him on some level, but the man's story just seemed too fantastic to be true. This fell way outside the realms of science. Allowances could be made for super-advanced alien technology; even Earth would have hover cars and laser guns one day, just like in the movies. But a boy that could conjure things out of thin air? Create tunnels and working elevators just by thinking really hard? That was magic, pure fantasy.

"I worried that the police would follow us down," Barton continued. "Caleb laughed, saying there was only one elevator. I said, 'Yes, but they'll *know where we are*, and they'll follow us somehow.' Caleb grew serious and pondered for a second, then smiled and said he'd put the loose floorboards back over the hole in the floor and glued them. I had to trust him, but I guess the police were utterly mystified by our disappearance. We'd literally been swallowed up by the floor. Meanwhile, the elevator descended for several minutes, which in elevator terms is a very long way indeed, even for old designs."

"So you're saying that the massive hole in the ground back there is an *elevator* shaft?"

Barton screwed up his nose. "No, not exactly. There *was* an elevator shaft there, but it couldn't have been more than four feet wide when Caleb and I used it. Now it's fifty feet across and circular. It's been . . . widened."

Widened, Ant thought. *Just like that.*

"I asked Caleb how deep we were going, and he didn't know, but we arrived eventually. We stepped out into a huge tunnel heading downhill—square and neat, clearly manmade . . . except it wasn't. Caleb had made it."

"Where did it lead?"

"That's what I wondered," Barton said. "It was very dark, so he lit it up with gas lamps—the part leading downhill, anyway, where we were headed. The tunnel was nice and smooth, and we walked for a while before I asked him where it led. He hadn't decided yet, but he suddenly smiled and asked if I wanted to ride. Before I could ask what he meant, we came across a couple of bicycles, one big enough for me. He took off laughing, and I had to hurry after him. We tore down that tunnel for—oh, I don't know, many miles I should think. In the end I stopped him and said we'd be in the center of the planet before long, and that was when his eyes got all big and round."

Barton shook his head. Ant sensed his story was about to get even more unbelievable.

"Caleb did his thing, and the whispering started. The lights just ahead suddenly went out. When I went to investigate, I stopped at the edge of the darkness. The tunnel now led into an immense cavern . . ."

He paused again, and Ant squirmed impatiently. He appreciated that Barton wanted to give him time to absorb the story, but these breaks were beginning to get annoying. "And?" he demanded a little more abruptly than he'd intended.

Barton didn't seem to mind. "It took a while to figure it out because it was absolutely black. I could sense that this cavern was massive. I was standing at the edge of a cliff. The tunnel we'd cycled down emerged from the cliff face, and there was a sheer drop below. I asked him what this place was, and he said it was a big, round cave."

"Oh—like a sphere?" Ant said, caught up in the

fantasy of it. He still couldn't bring himself to truly *believe* it, but he figured Barton had a point to all this.

"Exactly like a sphere. I asked Caleb to give us some light. 'Light the whole place up so I can see,' I told him. And he did. It was blinding. Took a minute to stop squinting through my fingers."

Ant found that his heart was thudding. "What did you see?"

"What did I see?" Barton murmured, drumming his fingers again. "Imagine a completely spherical cavern with smooth walls all around. Imagine that it's three miles across."

"Three *miles*?"

"Between the elevator shaft and the downward sloping tunnel, we must have descended at least a mile and a half. This place, this spherical inner world, had to be sitting right below the surface. Imagine a miniature sun at its center, just hanging there." He turned to Ant with a wide-eyed look of awe. "It looks the same size as the sun as we see it in the sky, which is to say it's the size of a coin held in front of your face . . . but since this cavern is three miles across, and the sun is suspended in the center, that means this ball of fire is only about one and a half miles away. So it's tiny compared to the *real* sun, but it's still a huge ball of fire. And it's bright enough that you can't look at it directly."

Ant said nothing.

"Caleb stepped out of the tunnel before I could stop him. But instead of falling down the rounded cliff face, he kind of *stood* on it. He stood there horizontally, at right angles to me. And he just started walking. I leaned out to watch him in amazement, and as I did so, I felt strange, like my personal gravity had altered. Caleb laughed at me and said it's okay, we can walk around the inside of his new world, even upside down at the top."

"He created *gravity*?"

"I don't know where he learned about it. I don't think he consciously grasped the concept, but he must have learned about it on TV in some form, something that clicked in his mind so he had a basic understanding of it."

"He created an underground inside-out world," Ant whispered.

Barton nodded. "Yes, and one that Caleb would spend the next few months filling with grassy hills and fields, a river or two, even a waterfall. This was a private world that nobody could ever reach, where Caleb could go wild with his imagination, a place he would be safe. We built houses together, an entire village, and started populating them with people. Not real people, you understand, but facsimiles, rather like androids. I could finally let Caleb run around unsupervised, teach him how to interact with people without endangering anyone, let him make mistakes and learn from the consequences, prepare him for the *real* world. Pretty amazing, I think you'll agree?"

"Yeah. Except . . . I don't believe a word of it."

"Ah," the chauffeur said with a half-smile, "but you will, Master Anthony, you will. We'll be there soon."

The winding road stretched ahead. Barton had the limo's headlights on full beams to better anticipate the sharp bends.

"Where are we going?" Ant muttered.

Chapter 12

Liam distinctly heard Madison gasp on the other end of the phone.

Then, tentatively, she whispered, "Where are you, Liam? Wait, never mind. Head for the waterfall, and I'll meet you there."

"*What* waterfall? What are you talking about?"

"The waterfall." Her voice was low and urgent. "On the hill near the forest. Just look up and you'll see it. Meet me there, okay? Hurry. Watch out for Caleb. He's dangerous."

"Why do I need to—" Liam started to ask, but there was a click and the line went dead. He stared in amazement at the earpiece again, then slammed the receiver into its cradle. "This place is nuts," he said simply. "Even Maddy's caught the crazy bug."

But the name Caleb gave him pause. Was Barton's long-lost son here?

Liam ground his teeth. A few things seemed a little clearer now. Caleb was, according to Barton, a very special and powerful boy. His involvement in this place remained a mystery, but there had to be a connection. Based on Madison's whispered message, she'd already met him.

So not a Government operation, then. Not a secret underground experiment. Just Caleb.

Before Liam left the phone booth, he attempted to call home. It didn't work without coins, so he ended up banging the receiver hard on the glass and then letting it drop so it dangled helplessly on its cord.

Leaning against the glass, he took a few deep breaths, then wrinkled his nose with disgust. The telephone booth really did smell like a restroom. He pushed open the door and stepped outside. All was quiet. He briefly wondered if the woman with the grocery basket was still in *Buns In The Oven*, then decided he didn't care. She was as crazy as the Chinese woman trying to sell him fish and chips, and the old man insisting that he wasn't interested in door-to-door salesmen.

Liam turned and looked upward. There was plenty of forest up there, and a long line of grassy hills. Madison had mentioned a waterfall, but he couldn't see any such—

Oh!

He stared hard. There it was. One of the hills ended at a rocky cliff, and a fine mist of water poured off its edge into a small pond below. From this distance, the waterfall looked like a solid white sculpture, unmoving. It looked pretty big, though, judging by the tiny trees that stood nearby. "The waterfall," he murmured.

He had no idea how far away it was or how long it would take to get there, and he wasn't sure he relished the idea of straying so far from the tunnel from which he'd emerged. He glanced down the street and across the rooftops, seeking the three trees and blackened stump. Between them lay the entrance to his tunnel. That particular area was pretty ugly, an expanse of scrubland compared to the lush green landscape everywhere else.

Liam chewed his lip. The tunnel was his only way home, yet as he stood looking across the rooftops, he knew he didn't relish going back into that awful darkness.

The waterfall became his primary focus, at least for a while. And Madison.

With a sigh, Liam set off. He could tell at a glance that the road leading out of the village would take him where he needed to go. He'd pass that abandoned car on the side of the road. Then he could either continue on the road around a ridiculous number of hairpin bends, or leave the road early, cut through a small section of forest, and follow the hills to the cliff where the waterfall flowed. How long would it take? An hour or two? Longer?

As he padded along the road, unconsciously following the white lines in the center, he wondered why on earth Madison had suggested meeting in such an odd place. Where exactly had she been at the time of the call? Why had she answered the phone at all when he'd been trying to call the police?

Questions, questions.

He wondered what time it was. The fake sun over his head offered no clue as to whether it was morning or noon. There were no street lamps anywhere outside the village that he could see, and he guessed it would get pretty dark at night across the fields and in the forests—

He checked himself. Night? This place had *no sky*, just a glaring sun in the center. How could it get dark? The sun was unable to sink below the horizon because there *was* no horizon.

It was pointless trying to think about it. He concentrated on walking, one foot after another. The faint breeze barely moved the long grass. The place was pretty, he had to admit—a picturesque landscape of rolling green countryside. It could be worse. Still, there was something surreal about the grass and bushes . . .

It took him a while to put his finger on it, but it was blindingly obvious once he did. It was all too perfect, too uniform. At first glance the long grass seemed wild, part of nature, but now he realized it was all the same length, the exact same shade of green, not a single blade out of place and no weeds to be found. Real grass wasn't that perfect. Real fields had high and low spots, grass of varying shades, weeds, dandelions, daisies . . . and insects.

Liam paused. It was true—there were no insects here. *That* was why it was so unnaturally quiet. There were no birds either as far as he could tell. No wildlife at all.

He continued walking. Even the road was perfect. The paved surface was dark and unmarked, not a pothole or crack in sight. The white lines were neatly painted—*too* neatly. Everything in this place was fake.

It occurred to him that the three people he'd met so far were also fake. He didn't know how that could be, but he knew in his gut he was right.

Robots.

The idea hit him like a thunderbolt, and his mind went into overdrive. He'd seen robots before, and had even been one for a while, but these were different. These were androids, extremely realistic human facsimiles with simple programming to make them act like ordinary people. The question was whether Caleb had created them. And what about this crazy inside-out world?

He drifted back to the secret Government base idea. Yes, this was an experiment of some kind. Scientists had found out about Caleb's superpower, whatever it was, and were using him. Perhaps he could create wormholes and nab technology from other worlds. If so, America might be far more advanced than it had any right to be.

Maybe scientists were testing lifelike humanoid robots and needed to place them in a realistic environment. *That* was what the village was for. Heck, that was what this entire *world* was for. The robots needed to learn how to interact with each other, how to live in a human environment. Maybe the Government planned to release androids into the real world aboveground, probably in foreign countries where they would walk among the cities, pretend to be real people, perhaps replace important officials and politicians . . .

Excited by his new theory, Liam was busy staring at the ground when the entire world plunged into total darkness.

Chapter 13

Liam fell to his knees with a gasp, his hands groping. The road was still there, warm and solid beneath his palms, but he was completely and utterly blind.

Then, a few seconds later, light returned. Not the dazzling sunlight he'd become accustomed to but instead a faint bluish-white illumination, barely bright enough to pick out the white lines on the road.

Moonlight.

He stared in amazement at the glowing ball in the center of the world where the sun had been moments ago. Now it was a full moon, growing brighter by the second. And as Liam watched, tiny points of light began to appear in the air all around, twinkling, slowly circling the moon. He had to admit it was a spectacular sight.

"So now it's nighttime," he said softly, climbing to his feet. He tore his eyes away from the stars and tried to pick out the distant waterfall in the darkness. "Great. Now I have no idea where I'm headed."

He did, however, have a flashlight in his pocket and knew the road would take him most of the way there. He would just have to continue and play it by ear.

He trudged on, growing weary. All sense of time had deserted him. He'd been sitting around the weenie roast just before 7 PM. It had to be midnight by now. It *should* be dark, yet it had been daytime a minute ago. Or a semblance of daytime, anyway. *These aren't real days and nights*, he reminded himself. *This is some kind of artificial world. Heck, maybe I'm not on Earth anymore. Maybe this place is alien-made.*

In any case, Liam had no choice but to pick his way in the darkness with his flashlight beam bobbing in front. The stars circled the moon in a lazy fashion. Liam scoffed at the idea, knowing real stars did no such thing. Still, the effect was mesmerizing.

He walked and walked. At the back of his mind, he imagined he would start climbing a steep hill at any moment, ascending the impossible upward-curving terrain that towered high above. The waterfall was way on up there somewhere. Then it hit him that he was *already* climbing that curved terrain; gravity just made it seem flat. He stopped, fearing he'd walked too far.

Looking back the way he'd come, he was shocked to see a cluster of orange lights shining high above the ground in the distance. That was the village, now clinging to a vertical landscape. He imagined himself as a hamster in a wheel, continually walking but remaining still while the world turned beneath his feet.

He flashed his beam around. He saw nothing but grass and a few clumps of trees. It was eerily quiet. Even at night there should be noises, particularly cicadas and crickets, an owl hooting from time to time. But there was nothing except the whisper of a breeze.

It occurred to him that he could try shouting. If the place was so quiet, maybe Madison would hear him.

"Hello!" he yelled. It was a weak effort, so he cleared his throat and tried again. "HELLO! CAN YOU HEAR ME?"

He waited, listening hard.

Nothing.

He waved his flashlight from side to side in deliberate strokes. Maybe she'd see the beam and come find him so he wouldn't have to find the waterfall by himself in the dark. "Where *are* you?" he mumbled.

Sighing, he continued walking. He would keep an eye open for the woods. They should start somewhere over to the right across the fields. Remembering what he'd seen earlier as he'd stood in the village looking up at the landscape, he needed to cross the fields, cut through the tip of the forest, and then follow the hills to the cliff edge where the waterfall flowed.

He remembered the car, too. It had been abandoned off the road just outside the woods. With that in mind, he simply needed to stay on the road until he found the car.

He picked up his pace, wishing his flashlight would reach farther ahead. In his own world, when the moon was full, he could see the distant hills silhouetted against the night sky. But here, with no horizon and no sky, almost everything was black. It wouldn't be so bad if there were more towns, street lamps, houses, cars, and all the rest of the stuff that made up the modern world. Instead there was silence and absolutely no sign of life except for the dim lights back in the village.

Liam squinted. He'd just spotted another light, a fairly big one, way over his head beyond the moon and slow-moving stars. Or perhaps a collection of small lights? It might be a house or a few houses huddled together. It was hard to tell, but it gave him hope.

Abruptly, he came across the car. It stood silent and motionless in the grass several yards from the road. He stopped and flashed his beam over it, and his jaw dropped open. It wasn't just any old car. It was a *police* car. A big, powerful police cruiser just like the ones that drove around his neighborhood. The front end was crumpled against a tree.

He went to peer in the side windows and found empty seats. But then, as he moved around to the front, he saw fragments of glass from a shattered windshield.

"Oh no," he moaned.

Steeling himself, he crept closer and circled the car, flashing his light low. After a minute, he let out a ragged sigh of relief. No dead officers. No rotting corpses. No skeletal remains. Whoever had crashed the car had been carted off to the hospital—or the morgue.

Liam shone his flashlight into the trees. This was about where he needed to leave the road and cut through the forest. Either that or keep following the road around endless hairpin bends. His head told him that the forest would cut the journey down and save a lot of time, but his nerves were advising him to stay on the road.

"In horror movies, people always stray from the road and get eaten by werewolves," he muttered, trying to make up his mind. The forest was so, so black. But then, so was the road ahead. Still, he clearly remembered it was a very *short* section of forest he needed to cut through. He'd be through in no time.

He plunged into the trees and began stomping around on brittle twigs and dry leaves. In a way, he was glad the world was so devoid of life. At least it meant he didn't have to worry about mosquitoes and snakes and other nasty critters. But he missed the lightning bugs and the chirping of nighttime cicadas.

His flashlight picked out spindly branches and clumps of bushes, which he tried to navigate while staying true to his path. If he didn't end up going off course and walking in circles, he should be able to reach the other side in no time.

A noise to his right brought him up short. He paused, shining his flashlight around. What *was* that? It came again, a rustling sound among the trees. Someone was there. Or some*thing*.

"Hello?" he called nervously, instantly thinking of all the scary movies he'd seen where the last thing a victim said before being stabbed to death was "Hello?" in a loud, quavering voice. He bit his tongue and listened in silence.

The noise came again, closer now. He pointed his flashlight beam in that direction, certain he would be able to see whatever it was.

And then he saw it, shambling toward him, a heavyset man with half his face missing and a slimy substance glistening on his ragged shirt. It wasn't the same man he'd seen back at the house, but he had the same horrible disfigurement and rotten-onion stench.

A Lurker.

Liam yelled and bolted. His chest heaved as he flashed his beam behind him, searching for the Lurker as he sprinted through the woods. He glimpsed the nightmarish shambling figure in the bouncing light.

Outrunning the creature and hiding somewhere should be easy enough, but for how long? What if it sniffed him out? What if there were others nearby?

He zigzagged wildly between the trees. Annoyingly, unlike much of the landscape, this patch was uneven and slippery with loose soil and dry leaves. On impulse, he switched off his flashlight and stumbled in darkness for a full half-minute, his hands outstretched. The Lurker couldn't follow him now!—unless of course it could see in the dark. It could probably hear him anyway, what with all the cracking twigs and exclamations every time he tripped and bumped into something.

He slipped around to the far side of a tree and waited, his heart pounding. He had a nasty coppery taste in his mouth. He stood as still as possible, catching his breath and listening intently.

A noise sounded in the darkness—rustling leaves, shuffling footfalls, not too far away and getting closer. Liam fought with indecision. Should he make another run for it or wait and see if the creature passed him by? He held on a little longer, trying to breathe quietly and calmly despite the need to pant like a dog.

The Lurker was close now. Liam's entire body tensed up, coiled like a spring, ready to launch into a sprint.

But then the shuffling stopped. A silence followed, then another shuffle, then silence again. Liam held his breath, wondering, *hoping* that the creature had lost the scent. Sweat dribbled down his face and tickled his nose.

The Lurker moved again. The shuffling grew louder, easily within twenty feet.

Liam pressed back against the rough trunk, his head turned to the right, trying to make out shapes in the gloom but barely able to see his own two feet.

A twig cracked. Liam thought he saw movement, a black shambling figure. The moment he saw it, it saw *him* and let out a low, mournful moan. The shuffling intensified, quickened, changing direction and coming toward him. Liam whimpered and tore away from his hiding place, fumbling to switch on his flashlight.

When the beam came on, he only just stopped himself

from colliding with a tree that had materialized before him. He dashed around it, glancing backward and aiming the beam at his pursuer. He glimpsed two wide, staring eyes just before the creature jerked and lifted a skeletal hand to shield against the light.

Liam ran.

Chapter 14

Liam lost count of how many trees he zigzagged between in his panic. He climbed a slope and slipped back down the other side. He tripped and badly grazed the palm of his hand, dropping the flashlight. He picked it up and ran on, the light trained firmly on the leafy ground. Assuming his mad dash hadn't taken him way off course, he should emerge from the trees soon.

He saw light ahead. Without hesitation, he altered his course and crashed through the woods toward the soft glow that silhouetted the distant trees.

Then he heard another moan. This one was loud, somewhere to his left and ahead. It couldn't be the same Lurker; it had to be another, coming to intercept him. Shocked, Liam put on more speed, giving the Lurker a wide berth.

It lunged out of the gloom, throwing itself toward him as he instinctively shone his flashlight at it. This Lurker had an eye missing, nothing but an empty black socket. As the beam played across its ugly features, the creature recoiled and staggered away, tripping on its own feet. Liam caught a glimpse of lumpy yellow flesh on its face and arms, but he also saw flashes of shiny white skull and bone showing through, too.

Then Liam was past, dashing away, his feet hardly touching the ground.

It didn't like the light, a small, logical part of his mind informed him.

Shut up and run! the rest of him screamed.

His legs kept pumping, spurred on by terror and adrenaline. He scampered the rest of the way through the forest until he burst out of the trees into the light.

He had a breathless moment to take in the brightly lit, cheerful burger restaurant with a sign that said 'All food FREE.' Then he noticed five more Lurkers lumbering toward him from the shadows of the trees a short distance away. They came for him as he stood gawking at the misplaced restaurant.

With no time to think, he rushed in through the glass entrance door and skidded on the slick, shiny floor. The place was immaculate, but then it probably didn't get many visitors. Surprisingly, a few customers were seated around tables. They refrained from glancing up despite his dramatic entrance, continuing instead to munch on burgers and fries.

The Lurkers clustered outside on the fringes of darkness, squinting in the light that flooded out of the restaurant windows. They looked like they were fighting some unseen force, unable to step any closer, their faces buried in the crooks of their arms. They *really* couldn't stand the light.

Liam tore his gaze from them and sought help. There was only one worker that he could see, a pasty-faced teenager with terrible acne. His name tag read Jonathan.

"What can I get you today, sir?" he said in a bored monotone.

Liam pointed out the window. "How about a machine gun?" he snapped. "Seriously, can't you see what's out there?"

Jonathan blinked, glanced toward the windows, and

returned his attention to Liam. "And would you like fries with your order, sir?"

"I'm not hungry!"

Actually, that wasn't quite true, but right now food was far from his mind. At least seven Lurkers were outside in the shadows, shuffling around the building, looking for something. Each time one came close to the glass, it squinted and recoiled, then tried to look in again, then recoiled again, and so on, over and over.

Liam would have liked to lock the door just to be safe, but the idiot behind the counter was bent on selling him fast food. After a while, the Lurkers slunk away out of sight, receding into the shadows.

At last, Liam turned to Jonathan and studied him in silence. The teenager looked normal enough but acted as weird as all the other people Liam had met in this world. Was he a robot? The idea of androids had seemed like the obvious answer earlier, but now doubt crept in. This wasn't TV. Jonathan looked way too human even if he acted weird.

Maybe Jonathan was a real person after all, but he'd been hypnotized. Or worse, *lobotomized*. According to the movies, surgeons in the olden days would 'treat' psychotic patients by severing nerves at the front of the brain. As a result, the patient was calmer but ultimately a vegetable, a shuffling zombie unable to string two words together. Liam had seen this barbaric process in horror movies he wasn't supposed to watch, but he'd discovered—much to his shock—that the process was based on fact. The so-called treatment had been commonplace until the 1970s.

Liam stared at Jonathan, and Jonathan stared back. There was definitely something oddly vacant about his expression. *Lobotomized?* he wondered. *Hypnotized? Or a robot?*

"Where did you come from?" he asked carefully, trying to be friendly. He felt as though he were talking to a child.

Jonathan stared back. "Good day, sir. What can I get you?"

At a loss, Liam decided this was as good a time as any to answer the call of nature. "Uh, is there a restroom?"

The server nodded and pointed. "Yes, over there."

"Okay. Thanks."

Liam walked away, curious. He pushed open the men's restroom door. Inside was a clean, white-tiled floor and a single cubicle containing a spotless toilet. There was a urinal outside the cubicle along with a sink and a trash can. All very normal. Liam relieved himself and walked back outside. He approached the server, who stood in the same place as always.

Movement came from the half-hidden kitchen area behind Jonathan. Liam noticed two cooks shuffling around doing mundane kitchen duties.

He glanced back over his shoulder at the customers. Four of them. One sat alone near a window, and behind him Liam glimpsed a Lurker hurrying past outside. The customer seemed unaware or uncaring of the ugly brutes. Three other customers sat together at a table in the middle—a mom and dad, and next to them a toddler perched in a highchair. The parents were munching on their burgers, talking amiably to each other.

Liam wandered closer. They never glanced his way even when he stood a yard from their table glaring rudely down at them, deliberately pushing boundaries. They continued their conversation unabated, the dad saying something about how the car was acting up and he'd have to take it to a garage. The mom sighed, saying, "That's all we need." The toddler, a cute blond girl, squirmed in her chair and started fussing until the mom put down her burger and offered the girl more of her fries.

Liam sat down next to the woman and stared hard at her. She didn't react. He might as well have been invisible. He edged closer until his nose was inches from her cheek. *No way she's a robot*, Liam decided, peering at her skin. No blemishes or pimples, but it looked real enough. She had lipstick on, a little eyeliner, neatly plucked eyebrows. She was definitely not a robot. Nobody could make a robot look this real. But the idea of a robot was far more appealing than a bunch of people who had been lobotomized.

On impulse, he scooped the woman's burger and fries onto the floor in one sudden, sweeping movement. It was so unlike anything he'd ever done before that it made his heart pound. He stood, prepared to offer a stream of apologies.

The man and woman stopped talking. The woman glanced at the empty spot on the table where her food should be, then at the mess on the floor. Then she smiled. "Oops. Naughty girl." She shook her head and wagged her finger at the toddler. "Be good now, Chloe." She reached for her purse and said to her husband, "I'll be right back."

But she couldn't get up with Liam standing in the way. She appeared to notice him for the first time and looked confused. She waited.

Liam stared at her, refusing to move. "Something you want to say?" he asked gently.

The woman put her purse down and leaned over the table to her husband. "So what's wrong with the car? Did you ever find out?"

"Transmission, I think," the man said, chewing. He wiped his mouth on a napkin. "I checked the fluid, but it looks fine. Old Sid next door reckons it'll be expensive to repair. Could be something simple, maybe the torque converter, but there's lot of labor involved in getting to it."

The woman sighed. "That's all we need."

The little blond girl squirmed suddenly, starting to fuss. The woman reached down to pick up a couple of fries, then realized they weren't there anymore so reached across the table and took a few of husband's. She offered them to the toddler, who chewed hungrily.

"So you can adapt," Liam murmured.

He decided to try something more drastic. He got up and, feeling rotten about it, picked the toddler out of her high chair. The little girl made no fuss, and her mom and dad acted like they hadn't noticed as Liam took the toddler off to the far side of the restaurant. He placed her gently on the floor. It was safer than letting her sit on one of the grown-up seats.

He returned to the parents, keeping his eye on the blond girl. She sat happily for a moment, then started crawling around. The man was busy talking to his wife. ". . . Maybe the torque converter, but there's lot of labor involved in getting to it."

"That's all we need," the woman said with a sigh.

There was a strange pause, as if something was expected. Sure enough, the toddler—from the far end of the restaurant—began to fuss. Her plaintive cries carried across the room, and the mom immediately reached for fries that weren't there. She picked up some from her husband's now mostly empty meal and handed them to her daughter—who also wasn't there.

A look of intense confusion played across the woman's face. She looked around, holding the fries aloft. Then she got up, following the toddler's cries. She picked up the girl, cradled her, and returned. Seconds later she was back at the table, and her girl was sitting happily in her highchair, munching away.

Liam sighed. This was all very interesting, but he was none the wiser. These people—and he'd decided they were indeed people and not robots—were obviously programmed to play roles as if in a movie. Either programmed or hypnotized, same difference. It all seemed realistic at first glance until the routine was upset. Free-thinking customers were supposed to come in, order food, and go sit quietly and eat. Or leave. Either way, there wasn't supposed to be any interaction with the movie extras. That was against the rules.

"What *is* this place?" he yelled, suddenly angry.

The Lurkers started thumping on the glass door.

Chapter 15

Ant sat up straight as Barton slowed and took a narrow trail off to the left, barely visible in the darkness. They'd only driven a few miles and were still far from Edensville. Nothing but dense, black woods lay all around, and now they were headed along a dirt track, destination unknown.

"Where are we going?" Ant demanded, growing frustrated.

Barton pulled over. "This is a very special place. We'll walk from here."

"Walk? In the dark?"

"It's vital we get to your friends before the rescue workers do."

Suddenly, Ant was interested. "Get to them how?"

Barton switched off the engine and pointed to the glove box. "There's a flashlight in there. Wait, on second thought, let's grab those new lanterns you bought."

He popped the trunk, and they both stepped around to the back of the car. The lanterns looked quaint but were actually just a few days old and battery-powered. Ant had bought three of them solely for the purpose of chasing down wormholes in the middle of the night; they provided a more even ambient light and could be stood on the ground or hung from branches. He hadn't even had a chance to open the packaging yet.

They each grabbed a box. Once the lanterns were unwrapped and the tiny battery protection tabs removed, the light they shed was pure white and surprisingly bright.

Barton locked the car and pointed into the trees. "This way."

He took the lead, pushing through the undergrowth as though he'd been here often. Ant had no choice but to follow. He couldn't drive, and anyway Barton had the car keys. If something happened out here, if Barton was in fact some kind of lunatic . . .

Ant quietly checked his phone. The signal was almost nonexistent, just one bar.

It occurred to him then that Liam and Madison had their phones with them. Of course, there likely wouldn't be any signal underground, but it was worth a try while he still had a bar. He dialed Liam's first, then Madison's, certain the rescue workers had thought of this already.

Neither of his friends answered.

Ant followed Barton through the bushes for about ten minutes, knowing he would be hopelessly lost if he tried to find his own way out. He stuck close to his driver, placing all his trust in the man despite the weirdness of the situation.

"Here," Barton said at last. He held his lantern over a rock. There wasn't anything particularly strange about the rock, but apparently it meant something to Barton, a marker of some kind. He squeezed through some bushes and sidestepped a tree, and when he raised the lantern, a steep mountainside became visible in the darkness. "This is it."

"This is what?" Ant said, his heart sinking. "It's just a hill."

"Ah, but not just *any* hill."

Though woods crowded the foot of the hill all along its length, Barton had somehow found a place where trees were sparse. The clearing afforded them a good view of the cliff face, which was far too smooth and steep to climb without ropes. It stood a few stories tall.

Ant sighed. "I think I've had enough of this. Barton, my friends are buried in the ground, and you've dragged me out here to the middle of nowhere at midnight to show me a hill you're partial to. It's made of rock, goes on for miles in both directions, and has trees on top. So what?"

"Actually, its only several hundred feet wide."

"Yeah, but *so what*?" Ant felt like swinging the lantern far and wide. Instead, he stamped his feet and kicked at a rock. "What are we *doing* here?"

Barton smiled. "Calm down, Master Anthony."

"Stop calling me that! Just call me Ant!"

"All right. Calm down, Ant. Come and look at this."

As the man turned and picked his way through the scrubby, knee-high bushes, Ant stood breathing hard for a few seconds longer. Then, intrigued, he hurried after his driver. "This had better be good," he muttered under his breath.

Barton paused by one of the few trees in the clearing, a very small and young one, its trunk thin. It stood very close to the hillside. "Notice anything strange about this sapling?"

Ant looked it up and down. He knew nothing about trees and had no idea what kind it was, but he doubted that mattered. He looked for strange markings left by aliens, or severe burns from a laser bolt, or hideous monster-bugs crawling all over it, or something else out of the ordinary. He saw nothing that struck him as odd.

"Consider its location," Barton urged, holding his lantern high.

Looking closer, Ant still saw anything untoward. Sure, it was close to the cliff side, but so what? Did Barton expect them to climb it? Maybe if they went high enough, one of the branches would allow them to step across onto the top of the hill. He doubted it, though. The longest branch, about halfway up the trunk, did in fact stretch across to the rocky face, but the sapling wasn't nearly tall enough to . . . to . . .

Ant blinked and frowned. "Ah," he murmured.

"I see that you've spotted the anomaly," Barton said with a smile.

"Um, yeah."

The branch not only reached across far enough to brush up against the cliff wall, it disappeared *into* it. The leafy tip ended as though cleanly snipped off half an inch from the smooth rock, though Ant knew in his heart that was not the case. There was much more to it than that.

Barton spoke quietly, awe still evident in his voice. "This is not just a hillside. It's a tunnel entrance. You see, after Caleb created his inside-out world, it occurred to me that we'd need to draw in fresh air from somewhere. I suggested that Caleb create air vents, and he started by extending the very same tunnel we'd arrived in. We made the journey together one time. He conjured up Luke Skywalker's hovercar from the original *Star Wars* movie, and we traveled up the tunnel to the elevator. All those gas lamps were still working, you know. Anyway, we continued onward and upward, into the darkness, using the headlamps on the vehicle to light the way, something Caleb got a kick out of." He gestured. "This, Master Anthony, is where the tunnel comes out."

"My name's Ant." He jerked the lantern around,

confused. "But there *is* no tunnel. It's just a cliff face."

"There's a tunnel, but it's disguised. We couldn't have just anybody wandering in, could we? The location of this exit point is, uh, quite lucky in that it's surrounded by forestland. But there was still a gaping ten-foot-square opening, and we stood right here looking at it and thinking that just about anybody could stumble in unless we hid it. So Caleb hid it."

"Where?" Ant asked, his throat feeling dry. "Are you saying he made it look like the hillside?"

"Exactly. The tunnel is right in front of us, and that tree's branch has found its way in, breaking the illusion."

Suddenly excited, Ant took a step forward. "So this invisible tunnel leads directly to where Liam's house came down?"

"Yes—except there's a problem I haven't been able to overcome."

"Such as?"

Barton knelt and picked up a rock about the size of his palm. "Watch."

He threw the rock hard. It arced through air and, plain to see in the light of the lanterns, shot right through the cliff face without a sound.

"See, it's an illusion," Barton said. "I can throw all kinds of things through this wall—and have done many times. Look."

This time he picked up a stick about three feet long and approached the wall. When he reached out with it, the end of the stick simply vanished. He moved it around, then withdrew it.

"No way," Ant breathed. "It ... it looks so real! Wait—is it safe to walk through?"

Barton spread his hands, the lantern dangling from his fingers. "That, Master Anthony, is the question."

Ant's mouth dropped open. "You've never tried? In all these years, you've never—"

"Oh, it was quite safe when Caleb first built it. When we stood out here wondering how best to disguise it, he created this illusion and then ran straight through it, giggling the whole time. I followed him through, and it was utterly painless. Once inside, you won't even see the wall. The illusion only works one way."

"So what's changed?"

Barton dropped the stick and stepped up close to the wall, his lantern held high again. He raised his free hand and pressed his palm against the smooth rock. "You see? It's solid to my touch. I can't pass through it. Yet the rock, the stick, that branch above my head, even the air itself . . . *everything* passes through. Everything except me." He shook his head ruefully. "When Caleb sent me away, he made the illusion real to keep me out. Real to me, that is. Hopefully not to you or anyone else."

Now it was Ant's turn to step up and raise the palm of his hand. Before touching, he said, "So all these years you've been coming out here to see if it's opened up again?"

"Right. So close, yet so far. Without being able to enter here, it's absolutely impossible for me to find my son's underground world. I considered hiring people to do the job for me, a team of explorers, but that would reveal Caleb's power. Plus it would be far too dangerous for them. I've played it out in my mind dozens of times. No, Caleb is stubborn. He won't budge an inch until he's ready."

"So what makes you think he's ready now?"

"Because of the sinkhole. Caleb did that. He widened that elevator shaft and brought the house down into the ground."

Ant closed his eyes a moment, feeling like his head was about to explode. "But why?"

At this, Barton shrugged. "I'm not sure. All I know is that something has changed. Perhaps he's grown bored and is wanting me to come back. Whatever the case, you're here now, and I need you to help me."

Ant nodded. "Well, let's try, shall we?"

He pressed his hand against the rock—and passed right through.

Chapter 16

"Can I get you something, sir?" Jonathan asked in his bored monotone.

Liam watched the Lurkers. They'd gotten bold and noisy, banging on the glass as if frustrated, yet they refused to enter. Most of them stayed away from the windows, shielding their eyes, but the two at the door were the most persistent. They at least had eyelids; the rest seemed so badly melted that their bulbous, staring eyeballs were unprotected, though why that should make a difference to light sensitivity made no sense. They limped and shuffled in the background, some extremely thin and bony, others large and plump. All were stained with something yellow and nasty, a thick, gooey substance that Liam couldn't bear the sight of.

He hadn't been sure earlier, but after studying the two by the door, it was clear their skin and flesh was literally melting off their bones like butter left out in the sun. These people were falling apart. As one of the Lurkers planted a hand on the glass, yellow liquid oozed free.

Would they come in? The two by the door squinted and recoiled, but then came again at the glass, thumping at it with disfigured hands. They were doing no damage, just making noise and smearing the glass.

Liam sighed with annoyance, knowing he was trapped until the pretend sun came back on, however long *that* might take. He frowned and cautiously approached Jonathan. "Hey."

"Can I get you something, sir?"

"How long are you open tonight?"

Jonathan looked proud. "All night. We never close."

"How long until morning?" Liam asked, trying to sound casual.

"Excuse me?"

The flicker of confusion told Liam the server was unable to answer that question. He tried something else. "You have customers out there," he said, pointing to the door. "Are they allowed in?"

"We welcome *all* our customers, sir. Can I get you something?"

"Are they regulars?"

"All our customers are regulars."

"Yes, but are they actual customers? Have you served them before?"

Jonathan glanced toward the door, his brow wrinkling. "They . . ." He seemed to struggle for a moment, and then his face cleared. "We welcome *all* our customers, sir. Can I get you something?"

Liam spread his hands. "Sure, why not. How about a cheeseburger and fries?"

Jonathan happily entered the order into his cash register.

On impulse, Liam added, "No tomato, though."

"No tomato," the server agreed. "Would you like a drink with that?"

"Coke?"

"Thank you, sir. Have a seat, and your food will be right out."

Liam drifted away to find a seat, thoroughly nonplussed about the whole thing. How did this place work? Was Jonathan planning to stay all night and day, or would there be a shift change? What about the customers? Were they permanent fixtures, eating continuously, repeating the same dialog over and over? How could they possibly eat burger after burger even if they were programmed to? And there was the toddler to think about. She'd need her diaper changed from time to time, right? For that matter, the adults would need to visit the restroom too, on occasion. Was that part of their programming?

Liam slid into a seat away from where the Lurkers clustered outside. He didn't want to see their ugly mugs while eating.

His food arrived promptly. The kitchen staff weren't exactly snowed under tonight. Still, this made Liam even more confused about how the place worked. Where did supplies come from?—the hamburger meat, the fresh tomatoes, the fries, the buns? Somehow he couldn't visualize a delivery truck turning up outside.

He stared at his burger suspiciously. It smelled and looked good. He lifted the top bun cautiously, surprised to find that the tomato had been omitted as requested. He had a juicy burger topped with onions and lettuce, a dab of yellow mustard, and a squirt of ketchup. The buns were smeared with mayonnaise. Everything looked normal. The fries were hot and fresh.

When he bit into the burger, he chewed for a moment and nodded with approval. Amazingly, it was good. And he hadn't paid for it. Jonathan hadn't asked for money, and Liam hadn't given it a thought. Free or not, it really was a good burger, except for . . .

He stopped chewing and gradually separated the food in his mouth. He swallowed some of it, then extracted the lettuce. Something was funny about it. It looked real, but it had an odd taste, somehow bitter. No, not bitter—just *weird*. Totally wrong. It tasted nothing like any lettuce he'd ever had before. Everything else was great, including the fries. Even the soda was cold and refreshing.

He pulled the rest of the lettuce out of his burger and continued eating, staring at the limp green leaf on his tray. How could everything look and taste so perfect except for the lettuce? It didn't make any sense.

After he'd finished, he felt suitably full. He deposited his tray on the shelf over the trash can and passed by the family of three, noticing there was still a mess on the floor where Liam had swept the woman's lunch off the table. He wondered who was programmed to clear it up and when it would happen. Well, since the Lurkers were still loitering outside, Liam was going nowhere. He'd have plenty of time to observe these restaurant workers and customers.

The banging on the door had stopped. Even the two persistent Lurkers had given up on him now, and they waited with the others in the shadows. Liam didn't like the look of them huddled together like that. They looked like they were scheming.

He sat quietly for a full hour, growing extremely bored. He hoped Madison was okay. She might be out there in the darkness right now, dealing with her own horde of snarling Lurkers, perhaps trapped up a tree or something. He'd spent so long trying to straighten his muddled thoughts that he'd almost forgotten she was in the exact same predicament and probably just as scared.

The customers continued to talk, but when their food ran out, Jonathan brought more. Four times he came out, twice for the family and twice for the lonesome guy, and each time the customers started into their burgers like they hadn't eaten in a week. But the routine was the same. Liam tuned out the incessant banter about the car's transmission and focused on the guy who sat alone. He was like some kind of old biker dude, dressed in leather and sporting unkempt white sideburns. He kept his eyes down, chewing slowly and reading a newspaper.

A newspaper.

Liam jumped to his feet, suddenly curious. He couldn't imagine a normal newspaper delivery service in this strange world. Or in the real word, for that matter. Nobody read newspapers anymore, did they? He sauntered over to the old guy and rudely snatched the newspaper away to see what happen. The man abruptly stopped chewing and stared at the table without moving.

The newspaper was fake. There was no text on the pages—or at least not readable text. It looked like a newspaper from a distance, but up close it was nothing but lines of typed gibberish. The text was in columns, nice and neat, and a large photo adorned the front page—a photo of a house with yellow police tape around it.

Liam froze. With his hands shaking, he pulled the newspaper closer to his face, staring in amazement at the picture. "No way," he whispered.

The house was his.

This latest development struck an icy chill from head to toe. Seeing his own home on the front of a fake newspaper like this, in this fake restaurant, in this impossible world, astounded and horrified him.

What did it mean? What did *any* of it mean?

On closer inspection, he noticed that the shrubs in

front of the house were missing. His mom had planted those when they'd first moved in, saying the property needed a woman's touch. And there was no deck out back. His granddad had built that with his bare hands. This was a very old picture.

"This was back when Barton lived there," he said softly. "And Caleb, I guess."

How long ago? He remembered his granddad had bought the house about twenty-three years ago, so Barton had gone by then. He and Caleb had vanished, leaving the house to be foreclosed on and put on the market at a rock-bottom price.

Caleb had been eight at the time. That meant he must be thirty-one by now, yet Barton had suggested he was still just a boy, that somehow he'd slowed time. That was impossible—but so was everything about this place.

Liam wandered over to the windows and peered out into the darkness, still deep in thought. If only he could get past the Lurkers and head for that waterfall! Questions buzzed through his mind. Where was Madison right now? How exactly had she ended up in this strange world? Had she walked out of the crumpled house and along that tunnel to get help? Or had she been kidnapped?

And had she really met Caleb?

Outside, the Lurkers stood looking at the restaurant. Looking at *him* through the glass. There were six of them. One was missing.

Liam knew instantly that trouble was brewing. Where was the seventh Lurker? Why were they staring at him like that? It was as though they were thinking, *You just wait—we're going to get you any moment now.*

"Do you have a phone?" Liam asked Jonathan. Maybe

Madison hadn't left the police station. It would be good to hear her voice again. But, as expected, Jonathan's expression was blank.

Liam hurdled the counter and shoved past him. He scanned the area, looking for a phone. There *had* to be one. He made his way to the back where two kitchen staff were busy, one dumping frozen fries into sizzling oil, the other organizing a cupboard. They probably did the same things over and over even if that meant a lot of wasted fries.

No phone.

In the farthest corner of the kitchen, in an area customers never got to see, everything was in shadow. The bright lights of the restaurant failed to penetrate the eerie nothingness. Liam halted at the edge of a pitch-black mist, straining to see into it. *How could there be nothing?* his mind screamed.

A feeling of panic descended upon him. He returned to the counter, swung his legs over it, and slid across. He glanced outside. The Lurkers were stalking toward the restaurant. This time Liam knew they meant to enter. But why? What was different now? And where was the seventh—

The lights went out.

The restaurant plunged into darkness, and the hum of refrigerators and freezers died. In the silence, the sizzling of fries in hot fat suddenly seemed amplified.

In the blackness, Liam heard the glass door opening, felt a slight draft tug at his clothes, and heard the dragging of feet.

He turned away from the sound and bolted, fumbling for his flashlight. It took forever to get it out of his pocket, but when he finally switched it on, he swung around and pointed it directly at the nearest Lurker. The monster was no more than five feet away, and it threw up its arms and staggered as the beam shone in its hideous face. Liam moved the beam around, capturing a sea of ugly faces in its light as he stumbled toward the restroom.

He knew he was backing himself into a corner, and if there was no lock on the door then he was done for. The alternative was to run like the wind and hope he could keep going. But it was too late; he'd already made his choice and was at the restroom door. He pushed it open, slid inside, slammed it shut, and fumbled for the lock.

His flashlight beam shook wildly, first with desperation and then with relief. He had never been so happy to see a heavy deadbolt latch. He turned it, and the lock slid into place with a *clunk*.

He leaned on the door and, in the beam of the flashlight, watched the handle turn and jiggle a few times. A Lurker threw itself hard against the door, making it jolt under Liam's palm. He stepped back as the creatures outside attacked, *thump* after *thump* after *thump*. Evidently one had the door handle held down so that only the deadbolt kept the door closed.

His flashlight wavered as he sank slowly to the floor against the cubicle wall. When would this night end?

Chapter 17

The creatures rammed the door for twenty minutes, trying to break it down. Liam trembled against the far wall, his flashlight beginning to dim and his last vestiges of hope along with it. If these things were going to smash their way in and get to him, maybe it was better that he had no light.

He watched, horrified, as the beam turned a dull yellow, fading fast. The last thing he saw before everything turned black was the door handle once again jerking downward before a barrage of bodies thumped against the other side.

He never would have expected the lock to last this long. Then again, as noisy at the Lurkers sounded as they threw themselves at the door, most of them were skin and bones—if that—and there probably wasn't room for more than two at a time. The lock held.

In total darkness, Liam closed his eyes, dropped his dead flashlight, and clamped his hands over his ears. The thumping went on and on, accompanied by occasional moans.

Then, abruptly, the noise stopped.

Liam remained on the cold tile floor, pressed into the corner, listening intently. Had they given up? He heard nothing outside the door but knew better than to check.

Eventually he slid down the wall and laid out flat on the floor, overcome by fatigue. He didn't care that it was a restroom and probably disgusting . . . although, as he lay there breathing hard, he had to admit it actually smelled cleaner than a kitchen.

"You're gonna have to wait for me, Maddy," he mumbled.

He knew she would—assuming Lurkers hadn't torn her limb from limb or eaten her brains.

Liam drifted off.

* * *

He awoke to a blinding, flickering glare and the buzzing of overhead fluorescent lights. He jumped up, gasping. The power was back on! How long had he been asleep? More to the point, what was happening outside the restroom?

He put his ear to the door and listened.

They might be right outside, waiting for him to come out. Or maybe they really were gone. They didn't like the light, after all. He peered under the door, seeing only shiny floor and bright light. He couldn't see any Lurkers.

He swallowed, one hand poised over the lock and the other resting on the handle. In one quick movement, he yanked the door open, swung his head around the frame, withdrew, slammed the door, and locked it. Then his eyes widened. The sight that had greeted him was still frozen in his mind like a snapshot.

Daylight.

It was daytime again. He'd been asleep for—well, he had no idea. But it was daytime in this crazy world, and that meant the Lurkers had crawled back under a rock.

Liam ventured out of the restroom, noting the sticky yellow smudges all over the outside of the door and on the floor. But there were no Lurkers around now. Jonathan was there at the counter as usual, bright-eyed and cheerful. There were more customers, too—an elderly couple by the window, two businessmen talking earnestly at a table in the middle, and three teenagers standing in line staring at the menu. The family of three was gone, and the mess Liam had made on the floor had been swept up. The biker dude was still there, munching on fries, reading his newspaper.

Business as usual, then.

"Can I get you something?" Jonathan asked one of the teenagers.

"Yeah." The lanky youth proceeded to give his order in a flat monotone while the other two stood by looking only vaguely interested. All three looked a little worse for wear, their faces glistening, one of them with a nose that had partially melted away. Jonathan tapped away at the cash register, then announced that the food would be ready shortly. The teenagers sauntered over to a table close to where Liam was standing.

On impulse, he slid into one of the seats just before they did. The lanky youth gave him a puzzled look and simply stood there, unsure what to do. The other two took their seats next to Liam, hardly giving him a glance. They began to talk about school.

"This is nuts," Liam said loudly. Nobody paid him any attention, so he climbed up onto the table and stamped noisily. The moment he was out of his seat, the lanky youth took it, looking relieved.

This caused Liam to stamp even louder. "Hey, everyone! Does anybody here have more than one brain cell?"

Nobody gave Liam a glance. Ashamed of his rudeness but feeling a little better, he jumped down and stormed out of the restaurant.

On the wall around the back of the restaurant was a large red switch marked ON and OFF in big, bold lettering. Liam wouldn't have paid any attention to it except for the yellow smudges everywhere. On impulse, he flicked the switch, then walked around to the front of the building and peered through the glass doors. All the restaurant lights were out, along with the power to the kitchen. Ceiling fans were slowing.

"Huh," Liam said.

As he stood there waiting, Jonathan walked out and brushed past him. The server headed for the power switch, and Liam hurried after him. "Hey," he said. "What are you doing?"

"The power's off," Jonathan said, sounding a little puzzled.

"Does that happen often?"

"The power's off."

"Yeah, I know, but—Never mind."

With power restored, restaurant lights flickered back into life and ceiling fans began speeding up again. Jonathan returned to his duties without hesitation, his look of confusion gone.

So it took him all night to figure out how to put the power back on, Liam thought, *and then about two minutes the second time. These things can learn. Doesn't that make them self aware or something? Maybe even human?*

The daylight improved his mood considerably, and the fresh air felt wonderful after the claustrophobia of the restroom. Liam checked for Lurkers as he stepped away from the restaurant and studied the surrounding landscape. A dusty trail led to a long line of hills. He nodded with satisfaction, certain the hills would take him to the waterfall where Madison waited.

Hopefully.

He wasted no time. Because he had slept in a pitch-black restroom for who-knew-how-many hours, he had no idea what time it was. Did this strange world stick to regular day and night patterns? Was it a full eight or more hours at night, or just a few? For all he knew, the sun switched off frequently throughout the day.

Liam rubbed his face, tired of the endless questions buzzing around in his brain. He tried to walk without thinking too much, but it was hard when the landscape all around reared up over his head. He looked down at his feet and jammed his hands into his pockets. The flashlight was there, dead but somehow reassuring. Maybe he'd find some more batteries. Perhaps there was a shop somewhere along the way . . .

The trail led him to the long line of humpbacked hills. He briefly entertained the idea of climbing to the top and hiking along the spine, running up and down in a cartoon fashion. The hills were somehow a little too picture-perfect, yet they *felt* real, and there was definitely solid earth beneath his shoes.

He saw a few trees clumped together and almost passed them by without a second glance. But then he slowed, frowning. The trees were identical, just positioned in random places and turned at different angles for variety. One was leaning slightly. Liam studied them closely, hardly able to believe what he was seeing. A single tree duplicated numerous times! Were they *all* like that?

"Am I in a computer program?" he wondered aloud. Here was a new idea. He was ready to believe anything now. If Madison told him he was lying strapped to a table in a laboratory being fed computer images through a rod inserted in his brain, he'd nod in complete understanding. Kind of like that awesome movie, *The Matrix*.

He trudged onward. He should have asked Jonathan for a breakfast meal. At least the food was real enough to eat. He was thirsty, too. The sun, as fake as it was, still felt as hot as the real thing.

The upward-curving landscape invaded his periphery again. In the full light of day he saw a cluster of buildings on the vertical face of the world ahead, which the main paved road eventually meandered past. He counted six house-sized buildings close together with a variety of smaller ones dotted around the surrounding area. There was a river, too, and a small lake, and what looked like the opening of a cave on a sandy beach. The beach was completely out of place in the lush green countryside.

Behind him, sunlight glinted off the distant police cruiser nestled within the trees by the roadside. If he'd continued following the road the night before, it would have taken ages navigating all those pointless bends—and he still might have been attacked by Lurkers. As it was, he'd cut through the forest and saved himself a lot of walking.

He scanned farther up the landscape to his rear and located the English village. It was now high on the curve. He'd come a long way.

The waterfall wove into sight ahead about ten minutes later. The hills abruptly ended at a cliff where tons of water roared off the edge in a foaming white spray. Liam hurried toward it, unable to contain the rising feeling of anticipation. "Please be there, Maddy," he muttered over and over.

The roar of the waterfall rose to a crescendo as he approached. He had to admit it was spectacular, easily a hundred feet high. He could feel the cool, moist air before he got anywhere close. At its foot lay a cove of clear water surrounded by rocks. The water didn't seem to be running off anywhere, but Liam guessed there was an underground stream and the pond was emptying out as fast as the waterfall was filling it. In any case, it was all very scenic, a perfect place for a family picnic.

And there was Madison, waiting for him.

Chapter 18

When Ant's hand passed through what appeared to be solid rock, he gasped and couldn't help stumbling. His entire lower arm entered the wall of illusion, disappearing up to the elbow.

"Whoa," he said, jerking backward.

"You didn't think the wall was really an illusion," Barton said softly, holding his lantern close to the sloping cliff face. "You thought I was making the whole thing up."

Ant suddenly felt ashamed. "Yes," he said miserably. "No. I mean, I half-believed you, but I guess I didn't at all, not really. I expected to lean on the wall and prove you wrong."

"Can you pass all the way through?" Barton urged.

The idea of sticking his face into an illusion didn't appeal to him. What if it suddenly became solid like it was for Barton? "What good will that do?" he moaned. "You can't follow me, and I'm not sure I want to go alone. I mean, how far away are Liam and Maddy, anyway?"

Barton pointed at the hidden tunnel entrance. "This is a dead-straight four-mile walk with a steep downward incline. And that's just to where the elevator is. Or was. It was right under the house, but now there's a much wider shaft in its place. Beyond that is a further six or seven miles of tunnel to my son's inner world, and that tunnel is lit by gas lamps."

Ant opened and closed his mouth a few times.

"I've had twenty-three years to think about this," Barton explained. "I once tried to drill my way through this wall. I brought a heavy-duty drill and generator, set it all up . . . and the drill passed right through the rock. My hand did not, and I grazed my knuckles. The wall is impenetrable simply by virtue of being nonexistent. And if I wanted to dig my way in somewhere else and hired a professional crew and expensive digging equipment— well, apart from the obvious logistical challenges, there's no way such a dig would be approved by the authorities, and there's not much chance of success for such a massive undertaking on the sly. But now that you're here . . ."

He looked expectantly at Ant, who sighed with resignation. "Well, I do want to find Liam and Maddy. But a four-mile walk in darkness? Through a tunnel? With just this lantern?"

"The lantern is more than adequate. Please, Anthony—see if you can pass all the way through, then come back for me."

Ant mustered his nerve and plunged into the illusion. He never felt a thing. Once through the paper-thin wall, he turned and found Barton still standing there as though no obstruction existed. So the wall was only visible from the outside? Freaky!

Ant waved. When Barton didn't react, he moved closer, holding out his hand. When his wiggling fingers were less than two feet from Barton's face, the man's eyes suddenly widened and focused. "I see you, Master Anthony," he whispered.

Ant withdrew. "This is so weird."

Barton jerked and straightened up, searching the wall. "And I *hear* you."

"Wait, what? You can hear me?"

"As though you were standing in front of me, yes."

"I *am* standing in front of you," Ant said. "I can see and hear you perfectly. But you can only hear me. All you see is a wall. Try touching it again."

Barton did so, and Ant watched the man's palm flatten as though he'd placed it on a sheet of glass that wasn't there. Yet Ant could wave his own hand around Barton's without obstruction, coming within half an inch of his motionless, splayed fingers.

"I see your hand poking out of the rock," the driver said, sounding hoarse now. "This is very strange. Clearly this wall is for me only. My very being is restricted."

On impulse, Ant touched the palm of Barton's hand. Barton sucked in a breath and jerked backward as if he'd just received a bug bite.

"What if . . . what if we hold hands?" Ant suggested, reaching through again. "Let's try."

"Be careful," Barton said.

While grasping each other's wrists, Ant pulled gently. His own hand moved freely, but Barton's snagged on the wall. No amount of tugging and twisting helped.

"Well," Barton said with a sigh, "at least *you're* inside. You'll just have to go on without me. I'll wait right here for you. And if I'm not here, I'll be in the car. You have a long walk, but it's an *easy* walk, all downhill. You'll come across Liam's house in an hour if you walk fast. I don't know what you'll find, but . . ." He looked troubled.

Ant stepped forward, passing through the imaginary wall so that Barton could see him. "But what?"

Barton gripped his arm. "Another two hours from

where the house came down, you'll find Caleb's World. I hate to ask you to seek out my son, but I have no choice. At least get a message to him. Ask him to let me back in, and then I can make the journey myself."

Shaking his head, Ant stuck his head through the wall and held up his lantern. Its light revealed a square tunnel ten feet wide. "It's a shame you can't drive me," he said. "The tunnel's plenty wide enough." A crazy idea popped into his head. "Wait—I could drive myself, right? What if I borrowed the limo? I could drive straight down the tunnel and be there in no time!"

"That's a fine idea, Master Anthony, but how do you propose we bring the car through these thick woods?"

"Oh."

"Short of fetching a bicycle, which would take time, I'm afraid walking is your only option."

Ant nodded. "A bike would definitely be easier."

"It's just a walk. And I expect the tunnel will become more difficult when you reach the house."

"All right, all right."

Ant faced the rock wall, amazed at how utterly solid it looked and how the light from his lantern played off its grey, irregular surface. He raised a hand, allowing his fingers to pass through with ease. And all the while, to Barton it was an impenetrable cliff face.

"Tell me why Caleb shut you out," he asked, aware that he was probably stalling.

Barton frowned. "Now? Time is wasting."

"I need to understand."

The man nodded slowly and retreated to the nearby sapling, where he sat at the base of its trunk. He set his lantern down and stared off into space. "At first, everything was exciting. We built the village together, basing it on a quaint little place I visited in England. It was a challenge, describing all the details so that Caleb could recreate the place. He did a remarkable job, though I'm certain a real Englishman would see the flaws in my design. Anyway, the problem came after six or seven months of living there. His imitation people started to deteriorate, and it became evident that he'd have to replace them every so often. He replaced them without fuss, but he refused to destroy the old ones. He saw that as cruel. I tried to explain that it was crueler to leave them alive when they were literally falling apart . . ."

"But they're *not* alive," Ant said.

"Well, no, but they did seem to have a degree of consciousness that I found disturbing. It was more apparent in their more advanced stages of deterioration. Their programming wore off, and when that happened, it was like they woke up and started questioning why they were there. I didn't like it, and the question of what to do with them became a power struggle. I wanted them put down, and Caleb insisted they simply be locked up."

Ant shuddered at the idea of deteriorating people walking aimlessly around a sleepy English village. *There's no way I'm going there*, he vowed. But he knew he would if Liam and Madison needed him to. What if they'd already headed downhill to Caleb's World? What if they were there right now?

"Nagging at Caleb to get rid of these people became an everyday thing," Barton said heavily. "It came between us. He just wanted to build new and exciting things and have fun, and there I was, the responsible adult planning for the future. I started thinking about doctors. What if one of us became sick? We couldn't live in isolation forever. One day I had an accident. I crashed a car—actually a police car Caleb had made. I took my eyes off the road for a second and lost control. It was quite a serious crash, and it scared me."

"Were you hurt?"

"Cuts and bruises. Mostly just shaken and thinking about what *might* have happened. I'm afraid I took out my anxiety on Caleb, telling him we needed to work on being more responsible, to build a hospital with working equipment, and a doctor or two . . . though I had no idea how that could possibly work. How does an imitation doctor with no real knowledge treat a real injury or sickness without real medicine? Caleb is very powerful, but he can't fix things. He can create, and he can destroy, but repairs seem beyond him. And I wasn't comfortable with the idea of him trying his magic on me."

"I don't blame you," Ant muttered.

Barton shrugged. "So I got onto him, and he said I was no fun anymore, and he sent me away. By that I mean his pet dragon escorted me out."

"His—his pet *what*?"

"One of the 'fun' things he created. I dread to think what would happen if that creature ever got out. It could, you know. This illusory wall won't stop it. Anyway, with Caleb riding on its back, it snatched me up in its claws and took me to the vent entrance, then breathed fire at me and made me start walking. I faced an exhausting journey, uphill all the way, and I begged Caleb to change his mind, but he wouldn't. I was angry and frustrated—my own eight-year-old boy treating me like that. His power had gone to his head."

117

"Yeah, he needed a good paddling," Ant agreed, trying to imagine acting that way in his own household. Even with a pet dragon to wield as a weapon, he would *never* dream of disrespecting his parents that way.

Then again, Caleb hadn't exactly had a normal childhood.

"We passed the old elevator, and I thought about riding it to the top," Barton said, "but of course that was a dead-end by now, the hole in the laundry room floor sealed up, so I carried on up the tunnel and eventually came out right here. Caleb was sound asleep on the dragon's back. He woke when we emerged into daylight, and we spoke for a minute or two. I admit I was too tired and angry to be the calm and rational parent I needed to be, and my boy was as obstinate as I'd ever seen him, so it didn't go well. I told him he would soon grow bored and want me back, and he said he wouldn't, that he planned to do nothing but have fun for the rest of his life. He laughed and said he was going to stay a kid forever."

Ant's ears pricked up. "You mentioned that before. Do you really think he's still only eight?"

"I don't know for sure. It sounds impossible, but so is everything else that boy does." Barton climbed to his feet again, picked up his lantern, and approached. "Now, you'd best get moving, Master Anthony. I suggest you find Liam and Madison, and then—if you would be so kind—find Caleb and pass a message to him. Tell him I'm sorry for being a grumpy adult. Tell him I miss him and want to see him again. Tell him—no, *ask* him to let me in again."

"I'll do what I can," Ant agreed. "But he doesn't know me. He might not listen."

"Well, get your phone out and take a picture of us

together. Once he sees that, at least he'll know I'm really up here waiting for him."

It was a simple idea. Ant spent a moment taking a selfie with Barton, making sure to hold his lamp up for better lighting. Then he turned and faced the wall. "Okay, so I guess I'll be back in . . . well, hours and hours from now! Man, it's going to be a long night. You'll have to square things away with my parents."

"I'll take care of it," Barton promised. "And one last thing."

"Yeah?"

"If the rescue workers happen to make fast progress and reach the bottom of the shaft while you're still down there, *don't under any circumstances let them take Caleb*. I fear for their safety if they try to stuff him in a car and whisk him off to some foster home."

A chill went through Ant. What about *his* safety? And that of his friends?

But the look on Barton's face persuaded him. The man had waited twenty-three years to see his son again, and this might very well be his last chance.

Chapter 19

The waterfall cascaded with a tremendous roar into the pool, creating a misty spray and yet barely causing a ripple on its mirrored surface.

As Liam clambered over the rocks toward Madison, he became aware of how dirty he was. His shoes, jeans, and t-shirt were covered in dark smears. He had no idea what his hair looked like but guessed it was pretty scary. And his armpits . . .

Madison spotted him and jumped to her feet with a huge grin. "Liam!"

They rushed toward each other and slammed together in a hug that lasted a full thirty seconds. Relief flooded through Liam's body, and it seemed a great weight lifted from his shoulders. He held her tight, fiercely refusing to let go, burying his face in her neck. Her grip equaled his, her fingernails digging into his shoulder blades.

At last they parted and studied one another. "Hey," Liam said.

"Hey," she replied, her black hair plastered across her face. She swept it back and absently smoothed out her *Tim Burton's The Nightmare Before Christmas* t-shirt. Her black leggings were splashed with mud and dirt.

"Where have you been, Maddy? I woke up and searched the whole house, and you were gone."

She looked sheepish. "Sorry. After the house stopped falling, I crawled around and found you unconscious. It scared me. It was totally black everywhere, so I used my phone to light the way, found the nearest window, and climbed out. I planned to get help until I realized how deep underground we were. I tried calling my mom, but there was no phone signal. Then I came across the hole in the floor in the laundry room."

Liam nodded. "Yeah, I saw that too. But you headed *down* the tunnel instead of going up?"

Tilting her head, she frowned and said, "I followed the light. Plus . . . I heard something weird in the darkness farther up the tunnel. A scuffling sound? I thought it might be a bear or something. I guess it spooked me."

The Lurker, Liam thought.

"Anyway," she went on, "I thought the lit area would be safer, and there had to be a reason for all those lights. I figured it was one of those cases where you have to go down to go up."

"That's a stupid phrase," Liam muttered.

They spent a moment peering around at the bizarre upside-down landscape.

"All I could think about was you lying there unconscious," she went on. "I started thinking I should have left a note or something, but . . ." She shrugged. "I pretty much jogged the whole way. When I got to the end of the tunnel, it took me a while to get over the shock of all *this*." She gestured vaguely. "But there was a cute little village full of houses and shops, and I figured there had to be people here."

"Right, so you headed into the village."

She shook her head. "Actually, I saw someone walking *away* from the village, following the road in the other direction. I took off after him. It was a police officer."

121

Puzzled, Liam let her tell her tale without interruption, how she'd jogged after the officer and started calling for him when she'd gotten a little closer. The man had ignored her even though he had to have heard. She'd slowed, suddenly wary, still following but keeping her distance. The man had stuck to the road but meandered a little as if drunk, occasionally tripping.

"By this time," she said, "I'd gone maybe a mile or more. I was all the way up there." She pointed high.

"I went the other way," Liam said softly. "To the village. So you never went there?"

"No. I followed the officer. The grassy hills stopped and became a desert, and suddenly it was really hot. That wasn't nice. But the desert was small, and we soon got past it. I was worried, though. We were coming up on the volcano, and the road cut right through it."

"Wait, what? *Through* the volcano?"

They both looked up, following the road. It did seem to go in one side of the mountain and out the other, but Liam had figured that was just an illusion, that it really just skirted around the edge.

"So what was it like inside?" he asked.

"I have no idea. Mr. Policeman carried on, but I went around. Took me ages, but it was pretty easy going. By the time I rejoined the road, he was way ahead of me. I had to hurry to catch up. And this time . . . well, I guess I was pretty fed up by then, and I went and tugged on his arm and shouted at him to stop and pay attention."

She paused. Liam said, "And? What happened?"

"His arm came off."

The image of a man's arm coming off in her hands struck him as horrifying. But now he felt sure it wasn't a real arm, nor even a real man. "It was one of those fake people," he said with a sigh. "Like the lady at *Ming's*, and the people in the restaurant back there."

She gave him a quizzical look.

He waved his hand to dismiss any questions she might have. "I'll tell you in a minute. Tell me your story first. So his arm came off?"

She went on to explain how she'd run away in horror, then realized the police officer had barely noticed his missing appendage. She'd gone back to examine the arm, which had slid right out of the uniformed sleeve. It had lain on the paved surface in a puddle of yellow goo.

"It wasn't real," she said with a shudder. "I knew that. But it was so weird. Even with a fake arm, that man should have at least noticed me! But he just kept walking. I followed him some more, and he led me to Caleb."

Liam sucked in a breath. "Y-you met Caleb?"

"Not exactly *met* him. I stayed hidden. I spied on him from the trees as that officer knocked on the door. Caleb answered, scowled, and slammed the door in the man's face. But the man knocked again and again until Caleb came out looking furious. He shouted and . . ."

"And what?"

"A robot came stomping up."

"A *robot*?"

She nodded and shrugged. "The robot took the policeman away. I was too freaked out to follow. I kept thinking I'd accidentally walked through a wormhole and ended up on some alien planet. It would have been easier to believe than . . . than *this*. An inside-out world? With zombie policemen walking about? And robots? And some kid living alone in a huge house?"

Liam blinked rapidly. "Hold on. A kid? I was seeing Caleb as thirty-one. Don't tell me he's still eight years old like Barton said?"

Madison looked him directly in the eyes and said, "He's eight. Or thereabouts. Definitely young."

"That's impossible."

"Well, look around, Liam. This whole place is impossible."

Liam hardly knew what to ask next. He started with the obvious. "What *is* this place?"

"It's Caleb's world," she said simply.

"And what exactly does that mean?"

Pursing her lips, Madison looked off into the distance, up toward the small cluster of six buildings Liam had noticed earlier. "I hung around Caleb's house and watched him through the windows. He made food appear out of nowhere. He looked at his shoes, which were dirty and full of holes, and flung them off, then closed his eyes and made new ones appear, all fresh and clean. And when he yawned, he stepped outside and looked up at the sun, and he . . . he switched it off."

"What do you mean? He deactivated it? How? Did he flip a switch or something? I mean, it's pretty crazy that it just goes out like that, but—"

"No, Liam. He just stared up at the sun, and it went out. Then the moon came on. He went inside and lay down on the sofa, and he took a nap. And I stood out there in the darkness watching the stars and thinking I was going crazy."

Liam stared at her. What exactly was she suggesting? Maybe she *had* lost her mind.

"When he woke from his nap about thirty minutes

later, he went outside again, stared at the moon, and . . ." She snapped her fingers. "The sun came back on."

She looked so serious and white-faced that Liam hardly knew what to say. He simply gaped at her.

"Then he went back to watching TV. He's all about the TV. He has seven of them in the living room."

Shaking his head, Liam flung his arms up and gestured all around. "Maddy, what *is* this place? What are those zombie people?"

"You're asking me?" She thought for a moment. "These people . . . There's a whole bunch of them locked up in a garage outside his house. That's where the robot took the policeman. Some are wandering around loose. I've seen them. They're harmless, just freaky."

Harmless. Liam shuddered at the memory of his night locked in the restroom at the restaurant. *They didn't seem harmless. They acted like they wanted to rip me apart.*

"These people are fake," Madison said slowly. "Not robots, more like walking mannequins. Caleb . . ." She licked her lips and averted her gaze. "Caleb creates them out of thin air. I saw him. He made a woman with a basket and sent her off to the village."

"He *what*?"

"Yeah, I know. Weird, right?"

"Okay, look, forget the fake people. Tell me about this place, this inside-out world."

Madison spread her hands. "Look, all I know is what Barton said and what I've seen with my own eyes. I don't know where this place came from, but Barton and Caleb found it somehow, and they lived here for a while, and then Caleb sent his dad away. Now I think he regrets it. He's bored and lonely. He has these fake people, but they're not the same as real people. And I think they must break down over time, so he creates new ones and stuffs the old ones in a storage building."

"Creates new ones," Liam replied weakly. "Look, none of this is making sense to me. Do you have any idea how *crazy* this sounds? *What* are you talking about?"

"I'm not crazy," she said. "But I think Caleb is very, very special. Somehow he's stopped himself aging, and he can do stuff that shouldn't be possible. He's dangerous, Liam. That's why I ran. I didn't want to go back the way I'd come, so I continued on the road and ended up at a police station. The phone was dead, but somehow it rang later anyway, and—well, that's where you came in."

Liam had seen a lot over the past few weeks, but . . . "A boy who creates stuff out of thin air? Creates *people*?"

She shrugged. "Caleb kind of screws up his face, concentrates, and then the air shimmers and there's a funny whispering sound, and then people appear out of nowhere. We need to get out of here. We'll tell Barton and let *him* deal with this."

"And how do we get out?" Liam asked weakly, his head spinning.

"Same way we came in."

Liam closed his eyes again. "You mean there's no other way? It's impossible unless rescue workers come down with ropes." He pondered for a moment. "Then again, they might have made it down by now."

He was suddenly filled with desperation. What if rescue workers had descended the shaft to find him in the last few hours? What if they'd returned to the surface and reported him missing or dead? They might never come back, and he'd be stuck forever!

But the logical part of his mind reasoned that they wouldn't just give up. The house was still largely intact and, with the absence of his dead body, it was reasonable to assume he'd survived and gone off exploring.

"The tunnel," he said finally. "Okay. If there's really no other way out, then that's where we'll go."

Madison brightened considerably. "Good."

Liam looked back toward the English village and scanned the scrubby area beyond. Though he couldn't pinpoint the exact location from here, he felt sure he'd find it easily once he headed back that way. But first . . .

"So this Caleb kid," he said. "How exactly did he end up in this place?"

Madison frowned. "Does it matter?"

"No, I guess not," Liam said. "I'm more interested in the things he can do. Or the things you say he can do."

The words slipped out before he had time to check them. Now she arched an eyebrow at him. "You don't believe me."

"I didn't say that. It's just . . ."

"Hard to believe? I know. And he's only eight. Imagine what he'll be able to do when he's fifteen or twenty! It's *scary* what he can do." She stared at him a moment, her gaze boring into his. "But you still don't believe me, do you?"

He chose his words carefully. "I believe that *you* believe."

Rolling her eyes, she grabbed his hand and started off across the grass. "Don't patronize me, Liam Mackenzie. Come with me. I want to show you something."

Chapter 20

Liam slipped and grabbed for the nearest bush. The spindly branch snapped, and he ended up sprawled on the grassy slope. "Where are you taking me?" he demanded.

Madison was forging ahead, scrambling up the steep hill. She seemed to know exactly where to find secure footholds and which bushes to cling to. "You'll see," she said. "I spent last night up here, looking up at the fake moon and stars. The waterfall's pretty strange."

"Look, okay, I believe you," Liam called after her. "Caleb is amazing and all that. I *get* it. Let's climb back down before we break our necks."

"Not until you *see*," Madison shot back.

Minutes later, sweating profusely, Liam made it to the top. His hands were grazed from grabbing hold of numerous brittle twigs. Madison was waiting for him, looking quite relaxed as she perched on a boulder looking down at the waterfall.

Liam winced. It was a *long* drop. He stayed clear of the edge and instead cast his gaze around. The hills stretched behind him, green and round, hump after hump. Ten feet from where he stood, the last hill in the range looked like it had been sheared off, a large chunk scooped out by a giant hand, leaving a steep, rocky cliff. Over this cliff gushed the roaring waterfall.

"So why are we up here?" he asked, sighing.

"Look around," Madison said. "Where does the waterfall start?"

Liam shrugged, studying the cascading waters. Then he frowned. "Oh, I get it. The water doesn't come from anywhere."

The more he looked, the more impossible it seemed. Near the cliff edge, a semicircle of rocks bordered a shallow pool. The falls started there, endlessly pouring off the cliff in a thunderous roar. Yet there was no source. The pool should have drained long ago.

But it was no more impossible than the rest of the place. "So what's your point?" Liam asked. "I already knew this world was like something out of a nightmare."

Madison spoke softly. "I just need to make sure you know how powerful Caleb is."

"What, you think he created the waterfall too? Come on. He's just a kid."

She stepped closer and peered into his eyes. Liam felt small next to her. She was easily two or three inches taller. "You've seen the waterfall with your own eyes and know it's impossible, but you can't believe a boy created it out of thin air. How do you suppose the waterfall got here, then? How did any of this place get here? And the people? Why did your house end up underground? What about those tunnels? How do you explain all this stuff?"

Liam thought about it before answering. "Beats me," he admitted.

Madison rolled her eyes. "Well, at least you're honest. My point is that we need to leave without him. He's too dangerous."

"We can't do that," Liam said. "Like I said, he's just a kid. If he's trapped here—"

"He's not *just* a kid," Madison argued. "He could make us explode into pieces just by thinking about it. He slowed time and stayed young! Trust me, he can look after himself. We need to get out of this place, and we have to do it without him knowing. Otherwise he'll stop us just like *that*." She snapped her fingers.

Liam chewed his bottom lip before speaking again. "Are you saying Caleb somehow made my house sink into the ground? From the surface?"

She nodded glumly.

"Then what's to stop him from bringing us down again? If he's that powerful, he could easily stop us from leaving with a snap of his fingers, right?" He still didn't believe a small boy had any such power, but his counter-argument made sense. "Look, we can't just head back without even trying to bring Caleb with us. How would we explain that to Barton?"

Madison frowned, then looked away. "I suppose you're right," she muttered. "Oh, but you have *no idea* what he's like. We just need to be *really* careful not to upset him."

"We'll tell him his dad is up on the surface, waiting for him. We'll take him to his dad. If he's lonely, then that's probably what he wants. Heck, maybe that's why he brought the house underground. Maybe he was trying to bring his dad down."

"I guess. But Caleb is kind of immature. A brat with super-powers. I'm telling you, Liam, he's scary."

"Okay, we'll be polite," Liam said, getting annoyed. "Can we go now?"

Madison turned to start back down the hill. "All right. Let's go see Caleb."

"Where's he live?"

She pointed to the same small cluster of buildings

Liam had noticed earlier on the vertical landscape ahead of them. "There."

Without another word, she began the climb down to the bottom of the hill. Liam hurried after her, trying to mimic her movements. He noticed how fragile the bushes were and how the long grass didn't so much tear in his grip but came free from the soil in an oddly unrealistic way.

Once safely down, Liam couldn't help noticing a vivid yellow splash of goo on the rocks at the foot of the waterfall. He grimaced and edged closer. "What's *that*?"

Madison looked away. "I think someone fell. I saw one of those fake people walking around with a huge dent in his head, leaking nasty stuff everywhere."

Liam wasn't sure what to make of that. Was she kidding? He opened his mouth to press her about it, but she had already walked away. He gave the sticky mess a final glance and shuddered.

* * *

Madison led them across fields to the road, which they then followed at a rapid pace. She talked nonstop, bent on convincing Liam that the eight-year-old boy Caleb was a magician of the highest caliber.

Overhead, the thick canopy of branches cut out the sunlight and forced them to walk in shadow. Unlike the real world on the surface, this place had no brightly lit sky to filter through the trees, just the greens of the fields and forests on the opposite side.

"So you think Caleb made all this?" Liam asked. "Are these trees real or not?" He rapped his knuckles on the rough bark of a thick trunk. These particular trees varied; it seemed Caleb had used his imagination here.

"He knows what they look like, feel like, maybe even taste like if he ever happened to chew on a twig when he was younger. I think his subconscious stores all the tiny details. But I bet scientists would be pretty baffled if they put a sample of his fake tree-wood under a microscope. Or a blade of grass, or metals and plastics and rocks. It all looks real, but it *isn't* real."

With a jolt of horror, Liam thought about the food he'd eaten. "I had a cheeseburger and fries earlier!"

She raised an eyebrow. "You ate fake food?"

"It can't have been fake. It tasted real. It filled me up like real food should. And it didn't make me barf."

"Interesting. Well, I guess any kid would know what a cheeseburger looks and tastes like, even what it feels like as it digests. Caleb and his dad had to eat, right? He made a perfect imitation of his favorite fast food." She paused. "Was it good?"

"Sure. Except maybe the lettuce."

She snorted. "What kid eats lettuce? He probably took a wild stab at that part."

The cluster of buildings that had previously hung sideways far above their heads now appeared to be sinking behind the forest as they walked. Liam caught sight of extensive grounds surrounding the large house in the center before the trees completely blocked their view.

As the trees thinned, they once again saw the cluster of buildings ahead, now at normal ground level. The house in the center was enormous, a mansion with a gigantic swimming pool. Another house stood next to it, plus four nondescript square buildings. The road swept all the way into the vicinity of the buildings, spreading out into a network of intersecting lanes. On the far side, the main road meandered off again, cutting across meadows, climbing hills, and eventually disappearing into the enormous volcano.

"Caleb Town is just ahead," Madison said softly as they passed a tall signpost.

"The house is huge," Liam said. "Reminds me of Ant's."

Madison nodded. "Twenty bedrooms. Most of them are empty. In fact, many of them are unfinished. I looked in lots of windows."

Liam squinted at her. "Not decorated, you mean? Or just not *there*."

"Not there," she said. "The house is way too big for Caleb. I doubt he even sleeps in a bedroom. He has a tent in the living room."

"Why?"

"Because he can?"

A one-story brick building came into sight up ahead, and Liam switched his attention to it. It stood back from the road and had the word 'POLICE' in huge stainless-steel letters over the entrance.

"Before you get your hopes up," Madison said quickly, "there are no policemen here. It's just a building, one of many unfinished projects. It's where I was hiding when you called. I found nothing but a front desk and some empty jail cells. The rest of the building is kind of a blank. I tried the phone on the desk, but it didn't work. I was pretty surprised when it rang an hour later, and you were on the end!" She stopped and turned. "Look up there."

Between the treetops, Liam saw a swath of land that he recognized as the hills and waterfall he'd climbed down from not so long ago.

"I was looking out the window while I was talking to you," she said, resuming her walk. "It just seemed like an obvious place to meet. I didn't know I'd spent the whole night there. And I didn't expect to be heading back this way in the morning." She gave him a sideways look. "I'm warning you, Liam. Don't upset him."

"How long was the night, do you think?" he asked.

She tapped her waistband, and he noticed her phone jammed in there under her t-shirt. "Only about three hours."

"That's all? It felt like a lot longer!"

"I think Caleb is a bit too restless to really sleep. He just takes naps."

At last they reached Caleb Town, marked with a grand overhead sign. They came to one of the small square buildings first, a garage of some kind. Beyond it, the mansion stood white and gleaming in the sunlight with dozens of windows spread evenly along each of its three stories. Twenty bedrooms? More like a hundred! The place was gigantic. What could a small boy and his dad possibly want with a place this size?

Liam swallowed, suddenly nervous. He had mixed feelings about Caleb. This world was truly surreal, full of impossibilities. Did the boy really possess some kind of magical power?

Try as he might, he couldn't bring himself to believe it despite the amazing things he'd seen in the last few weeks. Wormholes, aliens, echoes of the future, multi-limbed creatures that could jump back in time a few seconds . . . Heck, he still had nanobots lying dormant within his bloodstream! But all that was *science*. Caleb's so-called power fell into the realms of fantasy. It just couldn't be.

"What's in here?" he asked, veering toward the garage.

"Toys," Madison said.

Puzzled, Liam walked in through the open garage doors expecting to see a mass of teddy bears and board games. Instead, he came across several full-sized futuristic vehicles that he recognized from movies. It was like a rich collector's man-cave.

"Michael Keaton's Batmobile from the 1989 *Batman*," he said, awed. "A bike from the original *Tron* movie. Doc's DeLorean from *Back to the Future*. This is incredible!"

"Fascinating," Madison said. "But they're not real."

"They look real. And that one there," Liam whispered, pointing a trembling finger at a slender machine that hovered silent and motionless above the ground. "That's Luke Skywalker's landspeeder from *Star Wars*." It had three engines projecting from the back, one to each side and one sticking up. He ducked down, looking with amazement beneath the long, open-topped vehicle. Impossibly, the speeder floated just like in the movie.

He moved closer and put some weight on the rounded front end. The vehicle bobbed gently on a cushion of air. "How is it *doing* that?"

"Because Caleb is powerful."

Liam barely heard her. "I wonder why all these vehicles are from old movies. They're all at least twenty years old." Then he frowned. "Wait—Caleb disappeared twenty-three years ago, right? I guess he hasn't seen any of the newer movies. If he had, he might—"

"We should get moving," Madison suggested.

He nodded. "Sorry. Okay, let's go find that boy."

Chapter 21

They left the garage and headed to the house, glancing around as they went. Not ten yards away was another square building. A blood-red robot hovered by the door, angular and man-shaped, broad at the shoulders and slender in the legs, no feet whatsoever. Instead of eyes, it had a glowing red visor that stared impassively at them.

"What the heck?" Liam said, stopping dead.

"Another of Caleb's toys. It's standing guard."

"But that's Maximilian from *The Black Hole*."

She paused. "I take it that's a movie?"

"Yeah, from the seventies."

"Any good?"

"Awful." He squinted with sudden interest. "What's inside the building?"

Madison answered softly. "Let's just leave it."

Liam raised an eyebrow at her. "Okay, that's like showing me a big red button and telling me not to push it or else. Now I *have* to go take a look."

"Liam, it's full of fake people. It's where the police officer was taken—"

"I have to see," Liam said. "Stay here."

Ignoring her complaints, he dashed across to the building, ducking low as if that might help avoid being seen by watching eyes. He wondered if Caleb was spying on him right now.

The building's walls, like the garage's, were corrugated metal, clean and new. The roof was pitched at a shallow angle. But unlike the garage, this building had no roller doors, just a small door guarded by the robot.

Approaching warily, he gaped at the inert machine. The whole thing was shiny-red and polished. Maximilian really was the only cool thing about the movie.

As Liam stepped closer, the red faceplate brightened. Whirring, the robot twisted to look at him. Liam froze. Then it resumed its position, its visor dimming.

"Some guard you are," Liam murmured, stepping past and approaching the door.

He turned the handle quietly and pulled the door open. When he peeked into the darkness, a pungent smell hit him full in the face. He gagged and reeled back, gasping for fresh air. "Okay, so maybe I don't want to go in there," he muttered, recognizing the awful rotting onion smell. He pushed the door shut, but as he did so, a hand reached through the gap, preventing it from fully closing. He yelped and jumped back.

The hand was human but yellowed and bony, slick with yellow-colored grease that dribbled off and spattered the concrete ground.

"Don't let them out!" Madison shouted, hurrying up. "Close the door. Robot—do your job!"

Without waiting for the robot to respond, she lunged at the door and squashed the hand against the frame. There was no cry of pain even though it must have hurt.

"Help me," she gasped.

Liam put his weight on the door but did it half-heartedly, squeamish about causing serious injury even to these fake people, these Lurkers as they were becoming. "How many are in here?" he said, panting as the trapped creature pushed on the door from the other side.

138

Madison shouldered the door again as the trapped hand wriggled feebly. "Robot! Do your *job*!"

The robot twisted its head to stare at her but made no effort to move.

With a final, vicious shove, Liam and Madison banged the door shut—and part of a hand dropped with a splat onto the ground. Liam jumped back in horror, his hand flying to his mouth.

"It's okay," Madison said. "They can't feel anything. They don't feel pain. They don't even bleed—see?"

The hand was squished and severed, but no blood pooled around it. It wasn't even red inside, just a sickly yellow color like a slab of butter wrapped around a shiny white bone. Nasty grease oozed out, and the powerful stink of onions made Liam' eyes water.

"Now, come *on*," Madison said, gripping him firmly by the arm. "Please try to focus. We need to find Caleb."

They stepped away from the robot, and Liam couldn't help noticing how its bright red visor tracked them.

"That's nasty," he gasped as a rising chorus of moans sounded from inside. There had to be dozens of them.

Madison tugged him away from the building and toward the mansion. "They're deteriorating. I guess that's what happens to them after a while. That policeman I told you about came looking for Caleb. I guess it needed fixing or something. Caleb just shoved it in here with the others."

Liam thought about the Lurkers outside the restaurant. "And some run around loose, getting worse by the day."

Madison put on a pained expression. "They're not real people, so don't feel too bad."

"You say that, but some of them are pretty smart. Not the fresh ones, but the really nasty-looking ones . . ."

They approached the grand porch of the mansion and stood on the bottom step peering up between the ornate columns to the polished front door, which had small inset panels of glass.

"I warned you not to go in there." Madison glanced back at the building, now a safe distance away. The robot appeared to have slipped back into its trance. "Actually, I assumed the robot would stop you. I can't believe it let you open the door. But I guess it would have woken up and done something if they'd all started escaping. Maybe it's job is not to stop people going in, just to round up those who are deteriorating."

"Let's find the kid," Liam muttered, shaking his head. "I'm still having a hard time believing any of this. One minute I think it's amazing, and then I think I must be having a nightmare."

The grand front door was slightly ajar. Liam pushed it open and stepped inside. He was greeted with polished wood floors, a ceiling several stories high, and an elegant staircase that wound up and around in sweeping curves. A hallway led through to what appeared to be the main living room, while numerous doorways and arches leading off both sides of the hall offered no clue as to what lay beyond. For all Liam knew, the nearest could lead to a tiny closet or an impressive ballroom. The mansion was so big that it would be easy to get completely lost.

The house was silent. "Uh, Caleb?" His voice echoed up and down the hall, but nobody came running. "Hello!"

"He's not here," Madison said, sounding relieved. "Let's just go."

Liam ignored her and headed into the living room. There he found a plush sofa littered with cookie and chip crumbs, wrappers on the floor nearby, and plastic soda bottles everywhere. No less than seven giant flat-screen TVs stood in a semicircle before the sofa, each screen dark and silent.

"Wow," Liam said. "He really does like his TV. I guess he watches DVDs?"

Madison shook her head. "Actually, no. He just watches cartoons and other favorite shows he remembers from before. None of it is live or even recorded. He just remembers, like he's got a DVR in his head."

Curious, Liam found a remote control and thumbed the ON button. After a second, all seven screens lit up, showing different channels. The volume on all but one was low, so there was a collective low murmur of noise surrounding a single blaring Roadrunner cartoon. The remote was highly sensitive, controlling only the TV it was pointing directly at. He brought up the program guide and found a long list of shows Caleb obviously loved.

He switched it back off and circled the TVs, then stared in silence at the power cords, which draped across the floor and neatly came together as one before plugging into a receptacle on the wall. "I don't think that's legal," he said, pointing at it. "Seven TVs in one?"

"There's no power," Madison said. She walked over to an empty receptacle. "This'll freak you out. I saw Caleb do this and laugh about it. Ready?"

Without waiting for an answer, she touched the receptacle's cover plate lightly with one finger. A flash and sharp bang made Liam jump, but she seemed unperturbed even though her hair lifted as if charged by static. She held her finger there a while longer and raised an eyebrow.

"See? He has no clue about stuff like this. He knows the TVs need to be plugged in, and he was probably told a long time ago not to stick his fingers in sockets. I expect he saw a cartoon or other show where someone stuck a finger in a socket and got an electric shock, comedy-style, hair on end. This doesn't hurt at all."

As she stood and smoothed her hair down, Liam picked up a magazine. Pictures of horses adorned the front, and the title simply read *Horse Magazine*, but the text was typed gibberish. Another magazine had a photo of a cow and was aptly entitled *Cows*, but it was equally unreadable.

"There were magazines at the police station," Madison said. "He's most likely seen covers like these, or can imagine them, but he's never read one so can't recreate the detail. Books are even worse, just a bunch of nonsense. Look at this one."

She passed him a yellow hardback. Its title was as ridiculous as the ones Liam had seen in the village book shop: *Book About Girls At School*.

"I see," Liam said, thumbing through it. "He's eight years old and has never read a book about a girls' school."

"Just window dressing," Madison said airily. "All these books make the place look a little more homely, don't you think?"

At that moment, they both clearly heard a muffled thump coming from behind a door just off the lobby behind them.

Liam lowered his voice. "He's hiding from us. I think he's in that room there."

He moved toward a door, noting that Madison made a grab for his arm as he passed. She missed, and his hand was on the door handle before she whispered, "No, Liam, not that one. That's his dad's office."

"His dad?" Liam said. "Barton?"

"His *fake* dad."

He paused, looking at her. "Have you been in here?"

"No, but I looked through the window. Leave it. He's deteriorating."

Still Liam stood there. Another thump from inside sent a jolt of apprehension through him. He imagined a realistic Barton lookalike—but how far gone?

"I have to see," he whispered.

Madison reached out and gripped his arm, digging her fingernails in. "Why?" she said, glaring at him. "Why do you *have* to see?"

"I just do."

Without waiting for her response, he turned the door handle and pushed the door wide open. Inside the room, slumped over a cluttered desk, was a man. As Liam entered the room, the pungent smell of rotting onions washed over him. It was enough to stop him in his tracks and reach for the door frame to steady himself.

"See?" Madison griped from outside the room. "Leave him alone."

Liam squinted at the man lying across the desk. Only the top of his head showed amid the stacks of papers. As he watched, a younger and barely recognizable Barton brought up his elbows, planted his hands firmly on the table, and slowly pushed himself into an upright position. He stared out of ghastly eyeless sockets, and his tongue flopped loosely out of his open mouth.

"Oh," Liam managed to say.

Chapter 22

Caleb's imitation father had seen better days. What was left of the flesh on his face was yellow and glistening, covering only one cheek and half the forehead. The rest had melted away, revealing an ivory skull and grinning white teeth. The creature had no ears or hair, and the eye sockets were empty. Liam spotted one of the eyeballs lying on the desktop staring up at the ceiling. Unlike real eyeballs, this one lacked trails of connective tissue and tendons; it was a comic book parody, perfectly round and smooth, lying in a sticky pool of yellow goo.

The duplicate Barton tried to stand but seemed unable to straighten his legs. Liam heard a nasty *schlooop* sound and a loud *splat!* on the floorboards, causing the man to stagger and fall back in his chair with the familiar thumping sound Liam had heard earlier. He tried not to look but couldn't help noticing a foot and part of a leg lying under the desk, a pool of sickly yellow grease spreading outward.

The stench was overpowering. Liam turned to leave.

"We're going to build a village," the man at the desk said between gurgles. "I spent a year in England before you were born, Caleb, and I want the houses to look English, not American." The man's words were hard to make out because he had no lips and his tongue kept slipping out. "I want to know how much detail you can inject based on *my words alone* rather than what you've seen with your own eyes . . ."

"What's he talking about?" Liam whispered over his shoulder to Madison, who stood wide-eyed behind him.

"He's not talking to you," she whispered back. "I heard this before, through the window. This is all just something Barton told him one time. It's programmed in."

". . . This is a test, son, to see how well you can listen and interpret what I tell you," the zombified man said, slumping back in his chair with his head angled upward. He spoke in a monotone, his voice breaking in places. "When I describe something, you'll need to close your eyes and let me paint a picture in your mind. I'll tell you everything I remember, describe it the best way I can, and you'll use that information to create an entire village."

"That's just freaky," Liam said, fascinated.

The imitation Barton threw himself forward across the desk. "You can't create *real* people, Caleb. That would be wrong, and anyway, people are very complex, multi-layered, rather like onions. No, I don't mean in the literal sense. What I mean is—"

"Let's go," Madison said, tugging gently at Liam's shirt.

He nodded dumbly and backed out of the room. Just before he closed the door, the man grew agitated and tried to rise from his seat again.

"Caleb, we can't have these . . . these *things* wandering around. It's not right. They must be put down. It's cruel to keep them alive."

Then Liam gently closed the door and turned to follow Madison out of the house.

"Did you hear that?" he gasped outside in the sunshine. He breathed deeply, thinking he'd never rid his nostrils of that horrible smell.

"He's just programmed to say all that stuff," Madison repeated impatiently. "Stuff Caleb remembers him saying when he was alive. Now can we please leave? Caleb's not here, so let's go home and figure out the rest later."

He gazed at her as she stood on the doorstep wringing her hands and looking all around. He kicked himself. Why was he being such a jerk? Caleb obviously frightened her, and she'd made it pretty clear she just wanted to get away from this place. And here he was, dragging her back to the house and poking his nose into places she kept advising he left well alone. He felt like a heel.

"You're right," he said. "Sorry. Let's grab one of those vehicles from the garage and head straight to the tunnel."

"Sounds good," she said, looking relieved.

Liam made for the dull-brown land speeder from the sun-soaked deserts of Tatooine. He'd always loved the *Star Wars* movies, and he guessed owning a super-fast hovercar was everybody's dream. It had no roof so was rather like a futurist convertible car with a rounded front end and curved windshield along with its three protruding engines. Caleb had thankfully included two seats as well as a basic set of controls.

"Get in," he said. It had no doors, so he clambered over the side and dropped into the driver seat. The vehicle wobbled and bounced like a boat as he studied the controls.

Madison nervously slid into the passenger seat. "I hope you know how to drive this," she muttered. "Maybe I should drive. I'm older and wiser."

A button marked ON/OFF glared at Liam, and he pressed it. The land speeder burst into life, its three rear-mounted engines whining and throbbing. Liam gently turned the steering wheel, and the speeder responded easily. Once they were pointing toward the garage door, he pushed one of the two oversized pedals on the floor. Nothing happened. He pushed the other, and instantly the vehicle jerked forward with a roar and tore out of the garage into daylight.

Madison screamed.

Liam was filled with a mixture of feelings and thoughts that made him want to shake his head vigorously. He was overcome with excitement and awe at driving this futuristic vehicle from a movie, but at the same time he knew such a vehicle didn't exist on Earth. Of course there were replicas made by fans, but none that *actually hovered*.

He drove recklessly between several small buildings, past the mansion, and out into the woods.

"Slow down!" Madison yelled over the roaring engines.

The scenery whipped past, and Liam fought to stay on the paved road as it curved and wound through the forest. He had chosen to continue on around the world rather than backtrack, so they were venturing into territory he'd only seen from a distance. Still, he judged it to be the shorter route back to the English village. And there were no pointless and annoying zigzags along the way.

Not that the land speeder *needed* a paved road. The vehicle zipped effortlessly across grass and dirt, bouncing on its cushion of air. Still, Liam tried to follow the road as best he could, avoiding bumps and ridges and jagged rocks for fear of scraping the bottom of the speeder.

The forest thinned and gave way to unusually rocky

ground in the middle of grassy countryside. The volcano loomed ahead. The road cut straight into its base like railroad tracks through a mountain. Why anybody in their right mind would build a road through a volcano—

But, of course, Caleb was too young to appreciate the silliness of such a route.

Madison screamed as they hurtled toward it. Though the mountainside rose all around in a gentle slope, the road remained level, burrowing deeper and deeper until the walls at the sides of road towered overhead. Before long, the speeder entered a narrow, arched tunnel. Liam eased upon the throttle, his sweating hands gripping the steering wheel.

They plunged into darkness, but almost immediately the confining tunnel walls opened into a vast cavern with bright-orange glowing walls. The road ahead became a bridge stretching from one side of the volcano to the other, below which lay a pit of steaming molten lava that bubbled and hissed.

So this is what an eight-year-old thinks the inside of a volcano looks like?

Liam jammed his foot on the brake pedal. The speeder slowed to a stop, bobbing a couple of feet above the bridge. They were at the dead center of the volcano. Directly above, a giant opening allowed them a perfect view of the blinding sun. Liam hurriedly looked away, blinking furiously. He fixed his attention on the bridge and accelerated again, gently this time, straddling the white-dashed centerline and staying clear of the somewhat flimsy guard rails.

"Has this thing ever erupted?" he wondered aloud, already feeling unbearably hot. He squirmed in his seat as sweat trickled down his back. "I can't see how a bridge would survive two seconds if this thing ever blows."

"Caleb's eight," Madison said. "He's probably seen volcanoes erupting on TV, but do you think he's ever seen the inside of one? Have *you*? He doesn't understand how things work, but I'll bet this thing can erupt if he wants it to—without damaging the bridge."

Liam thought about that. "Where does all the smoke go?"

Madison had no answer.

They reached the far side where the bridge once more became a road. They plunged into a short tunnel cut into the cavernous wall and, seconds later, emerged into daylight on the far side of the volcano.

Moving at a more moderate pace, Liam navigated the road and cut corners wherever possible. Ahead, high on the curved terrain, he saw a familiar expanse of scrub and ferns. Nearby stood the English village where its houses and shops hung sideways on the slopes.

Liam grinned. They would be at the tunnel—the way out!—in just a few minutes at the rate they were moving. He squinted. *There!* He could see the three trees clumped together, and the blackened stump. His escape route was there.

He pressed down on the throttle, and the engines responded with a burst of power, causing his head to snap back against the headrest.

The curving road cut across a patch of desert inexplicably nestled in the middle of green fields. He made a beeline for a distant point where the road rose over a hill. The land speeder bounced softly as it sped across the dunes, and for a moment Liam imagined himself on

149

the planet of Tatooine where Luke Skywalker had grown up.

He sighed. Nobody would ever believe his story when he eventually made it back home. He wished he had a camera to take some pictures.

Madison had hers, though. "Take a picture!" he yelled over the noise of the engines.

She shook her head, her knuckles white where she gripped the dashboard.

Liam was certain rescue workers or investigators would want to find out where he'd been, and then the truth about this incredible world would be revealed. The place was scary and impossible, but it was also spectacular and—

His eyes widened. As he shot out of the desert and onto a grassy hill to rejoin the road, he saw a small figure standing right where his familiar tunnel entrance lay.

He nudged Madison. "Look. I see someone."

It took a moment for Madison to spot the figure. Then she sighed. "It's Caleb."

Chapter 23

Ant plodded along, already bored with the journey.

He'd started out fearful. The idea of walking an hour or so into the depths of the planet with nothing but a single lantern had filled him with anxiety. The lantern reportedly had a long battery life, but what if he dropped the thing and smashed it? Anything could happen, and then he'd be stranded in total darkness.

As time passed, his stress about what might go wrong turned into a longing for something more interesting. The tunnel was utterly featureless, ten feet square and carved out of rock. He had absolutely nothing to look at except his own two feet as they marched on and on.

"If only I had my bike," he muttered time and time again. Why hadn't Barton thought of that before bringing him here? They'd actually been home and could have thrown it in the trunk! This was the difference between adults and children. Adults just didn't *think*. If Ant had planned this trip with Liam, there would have been no question at all about bringing their bikes. They could have rocketed down the tunnel and been at the bottom in no time.

Of course, coming back up would have been a chore.

A gentle draft tugged at his clothes, pushing him onward down the slope. He wasn't sure exactly why it was such a strong draft. Was there a fan somewhere farther down, sucking the air in? Or was this just another of Caleb's fanciful ideas about how life should work? He'd turned the tunnel into a vent to draw in fresh air, and by golly it worked just the way he imagined.

Assuming Barton hadn't embellished his story, then Caleb was a force to be reckoned with. A boy like that had no business existing. People shouldn't be able to create stuff out of thin air or carve perfect tunnels through solid rock just by thinking about it.

How did he do it? Ant didn't believe in magic, at least not in the traditional sense. He'd read many times how humans muddled through life using only about ten percent of their brain power, and the theory went that mankind would be far more mentally advanced if they could tap into the unused parts of the cerebral cortex. It was all complete fantasy, of course, the stuff of science fiction . . . but an interesting idea all the same. Did scientists really know what they were talking about? What about people with documented special powers like telekinesis? Ant liked to think such powers existed, but if so, then it meant humans were far more mysterious than scientists understood. What if Caleb—

He heard a noise ahead, and he slowed, holding up the lantern as if that would make a difference. Its ambient light, though strong, failed to illuminate farther than twenty feet ahead. He stopped and listened.

It sounded like something flopping about. Maybe an animal? He felt a chill, knowing that anything could have wandered into the tunnel if they weren't deterred by the fact that part of the mountainside was an illusion. Heck, a blind man could have walked in and been none the wiser.

He saw no droppings, though. Rats and rodents taking up residence in this hidden tunnel would have left a mess, yet the floor was utterly clean. Maybe animals knew better than to explore an unnatural tunnel like this. Or maybe Caleb had cast a spell on it to keep critters out.

So what was the noise?

Steeling himself, Ant edged forward, straining to see ahead.

After ten paces, he caught a glimpse of movement. Something fairly large lying on the floor, thrashing its limbs in a lazy way, perhaps weakened by injury.

Ant moved closer, trembling all over, the light from his lantern jiggling wildly.

Whatever it was spotted him and moaned. Ant sucked in a breath, certain it was the sound of a person rather than an animal. With a sudden jolt of horror, he rushed forward, saying, "Liam? Maddy? Is that you?"

He stopped dead again, now standing over the prone figure. It wasn't either of his friends, but it was definitely human. A man with a ghastly face, staring eyes and glistening, melted flesh, and a lipless mouth that revealed a toothy grimace. The man's legs appeared to be broken in several places, disjointed and angled funny, its feet turned the wrong way. He was lying on his back, flopping his arms about in a feeble attempt to turn over.

Not human, Ant told himself, remembering what Barton had said. *One of Caleb's fake people. A walking mannequin.*

The smell was horrible, the stench of rotting onions. The imitation man was in a bad way. And just beyond, yellow smears adorned the tunnel floor, a zigzagging trail showing where he'd staggered up the tunnel and finally fallen.

Ant backed away, appalled. It would have been much worse had the man been real, with scarlet blood instead of that oozing yellow stuff, but he was still a pretty awful sight. His hands didn't quite look real. Where the flesh had melted away, the finger bones looked unreal, just various white segments that looked more like short plastic rods than actual bones, apparently joined by tiny gaps of air.

Recognizing this detail, Ant relaxed a little. *He's not human*, he told himself. *He's just an android falling apart.*

He made to go around, keeping close to the wall, but the man followed his gaze and seemed to reach for him. Then he spoke. *"Kill meeeee . . ."*

Ant let out a cry and almost bolted onward down the tunnel. Instead, he flattened himself against the wall and panted hard as the deteriorating man repeated the same thing over and over.

"I can't!" Ant shouted. "I don't have anything to—I mean, if I had a knife or something—"

He knew in his heart that he couldn't do anything even if he had a knife. In fact, he was glad he had no weapons so he wouldn't have to make that choice. But the melting creature was insistent, continuing with the wailing mantra the whole time. *"Kill meeeee . . . kill meeeee . . ."*

Ant sidled past and hurried on. But the man's pitiful cries haunted him, and he stopped and turned back, chewing his lip and wishing he had a strong enough heart to put the thing out of its misery.

It's not human. It's okay to end its life. It's not even life as such.

Telling himself it was a mere machine with a lifelike fleshy covering, he returned and stood over the man, trembling hard.

It's not a 'he' but an 'it,' a shop-window mannequin

animated by magic. It wants to be shut down. It's not human, it's not human.

He moved closer. The mantra rose in volume, the man's arms flailing wildly now. It seemed desperate. It would die right here with or without Ant's help, and it might be days or weeks before it finally melted away into a pool of goo. What kind of fate was that for anything possessing even the slightest hint of consciousness?

It's not consciousness, just programming.

As the man's cries grew more high-pitched, Ant swallowed, ground his teeth together, raised a foot—and slammed it down on the thing's face.

The head split open, releasing a huge puddle of thick, bright-yellow liquid. Nothing else, just a sticky mess. Ant gagged and threw himself backward.

To his relief, the arms stopped flopping, and the cries cut off. The thing slowly became still as the yellow puddle spread like spilled paint.

"See, not human," Ant gasped, sweat dribbling down his face.

He hurried onward, shuddering uncontrollably, his lantern jiggling in his outstretched hand. He scraped his shoe on the ground a few times, glad that the goo had only smeared the underside.

It was at least fifteen minutes before he was able to let out a sigh and truly put the ghastly experience behind him. "No more excitement," he muttered. "Just a boring tunnel would be nice from now on, thank you very much."

But he had to wonder: If just one of Caleb's imitation people had affected him so much, how were his friends were doing in a world full of them?

Chapter 24

Liam steered off the road and plowed through tall ferns toward three trees that formed a triangle. He slowed to a halt just a couple of yards from Caleb, released his iron grip on the steering wheel, and jabbed the red ON/OFF button. The whine of the engines abruptly died.

The silence was eerie. Liam stared through the windshield at the small boy standing at the perimeter of the gaping tunnel entrance. A large area of ferns around the entrance had been trampled completely flat.

Sitting motionless in the passenger seat next to Liam, Madison wore a white-faced, panic-stricken expression. In an attempt to mask his own apprehension, he calmly climbed out of the vehicle and jumped down onto soft soil.

Liam faced the boy and grinned. "How's it going?"

The boy stared at him. He had somewhat greasy, unkempt blond hair and a smudge of dirt on his cheek. His clothing was wrinkled, unclean, and a few sizes too small. In contrast, his tennis shoes were spotless except for scuffs on the front. Liam guessed that this all-powerful eight-year-old boy hated taking baths and had no interest in fresh laundry as long as he was comfortable. No doubt he'd replaced his shoes only so they wouldn't hurt his toes.

The boy spoke softly, keeping his head dipped and peering at Liam through low-hanging hair. "Where's my dad?" he said.

"Your dad? He's up on the surface." Liam pointed to the tunnel.

"Who are you?"

"I'm Liam, and this is Madison."

"Why are you here and not my dad? I wanted *him*, not you."

Liam pointed again. "Come with us, and we'll take you to him."

Caleb scowled. "It's not safe up there. That's why I dragged the house down here." He glanced over his shoulder. "Tried to, anyway. It must have gotten stuck."

"You . . . you *dragged* your house down?" Liam repeated. Though Madison had already put that forward as a theory, it didn't mean he'd accepted it.

Grinning suddenly, Caleb's eyes shone as he waved his arms about. "I should have done it ages ago! It's much easier dragging things down here than making stuff up. It takes me all day to make a house. Do you know how long it took to drag my house down?"

Liam and Madison said nothing.

"About two minutes!" Caleb yelled triumphantly, stamping his foot to punctuate his point. "So from now on, instead of spending ages imagining stuff, I'm just going to make holes in the ground and drag stuff down. Much easier." He frowned. "So where's my dad?"

"Um," Liam said, finding his throat had gone dry, "he's still up top. He wasn't in the house when you, uh . . . when you dragged it down."

"So where was he?"

"Outside."

Caleb rolled his eyes. "Well, *duh*. If he wasn't inside, he must have been outside, obviously!"

"Yeah, Liam," Madison murmured, nudging him. "Obviously."

"Who *are* you people?" Caleb asked, narrowing his eyes.

Liam thought for a moment and decided to take the honest approach. "We're good friends of your dad."

"Liar."

"It's true. Your dad doesn't live in that house anymore. I do."

"Liar."

Gritting his teeth, Liam said firmly, "Your dad lives somewhere else now."

"Where?"

"I—I don't know," Liam said truthfully, unable to contain his surprise. Where *did* Barton live? At Ant's house? Or somewhere nearby? Did he keep the car the entire time in case Ant needed him urgently? Liam kicked himself for being so vacant when it came to Ant's faithful chauffeur.

"So *you* live in my house now?" Caleb demanded.

"Well, I did until you dragged it underground." Seeing Caleb's scowl deepen, he hurried on. "But we know Barton well. Your dad, I mean. We were having a weenie roast just before it happened. He's probably at the other end of this tunnel right now, waiting."

Caleb pouted and folded his arms. "Liar. My dad's name isn't Barton. It's Hugh."

"He changed it," Madison broke in. "To avoid the police."

"I don't believe you."

Liam felt his temper rising. "We don't care."

Madison touched his arm and said to Caleb, "What he

means is, it doesn't matter if you believe us or not because all you need to do is come with us to the surface and see for yourself."

As wary as she was, Liam couldn't help being underwhelmed with the eight-year-old boy and his supposed magical power. He was nothing but a brat. And, seeing him standing here like this with his dirty, ill-fitting clothes, Liam couldn't help feeling sorry for him. How long had he been alone in this place? Twenty-three years? How was that even possible?

"Why are you still eight?" he asked as Caleb chewed his lip and pondered over what Madison had said. "You've been gone ages. Years and years. How come you haven't aged?"

Caleb allowed himself a proud smile. "I made time whizz by outside so the police would stop looking for Daddy quicker."

Just like that, Liam thought with a sideways glance at Madison.

"How could you possibly make time whizz by outside?" he exclaimed, waving his hands around and gesturing to the vast, sweeping landscape over their heads. "What *is* this place? How is any of it possible? What—"

"I made it," Caleb said.

Liam sighed. "Of course you did. Seriously, how did you find this place? How have you not aged? None of this makes sense. What are those fake people? Why are they falling apart?"

Caleb looked away. "I'm supposed to put them down, but I don't want to. It's cruel to hurt people. When I was little, my dog wouldn't stop barking, so I sealed up his mouth just for a few minutes to teach him a lesson. But he died, and Mom shouted at me and said I was cruel. So I've never hurt any animal since, or any person either."

"You sealed up your dog's mouth? With tape or something?"

"No, I just sealed it up," Caleb explained. "Made his mouth disappear. I think I made his nose disappear as well, though. He couldn't breathe after that."

Liam felt Madison's grip on his arm tighten. He decided to brush over the details of Caleb's horrifying story. "Okay, but look, those fake people are . . . well, fake. They're not real people. They're like mannequins. I don't know how they're walking about, but if there's a way to switch them off—"

"Can't you just make them disappear?" Madison interrupted, her voice soft. "You made them appear out of nowhere, right? So make them disappear. Or fix them, make them new again."

Caleb shook his head firmly. "Can't. I can create things, but I can't uncreate things. Or fix them. I can only explode them into pieces."

Create things, Liam thought with a heavy dose of skepticism. *Yeah, right.* Whatever this weird inner world was, it just had to be something altogether more scientific than a place conjured from the brain of a child. The cheeseburger and fries he'd eaten earlier had tasted too good to be fake. His bet was on an alien experiment. And everything in this place was part of it, including Caleb himself. What Madison had witnessed when she'd arrived—Caleb conjuring a new shopkeeper—had to have been startling, but so was a wormhole. That shopkeeper had obviously arrived via a wormhole, magically appearing out of nowhere. With that in mind, it was easy to see why a small boy would assume he had special powers.

"You don't believe me," Caleb said, glaring at him.

Liam couldn't help squirming. "It's just . . . Look, people don't create things out of nothing, okay? I know you think you're powerful, but you're not. You're just a kid."

"Liam," Madison whispered. "What are you doing?"

"It's okay," he said quietly. "There's a lot here we don't understand, but I'm pretty sure Caleb is ordinary. He might have a communicator in his skin. Whenever he conjures something up, aliens beam it down to his location. So when he creates a shopkeeper, they . . . they dress an android and . . ."

His logic was already beginning to unravel. These unseen aliens had androids standing by, ready to garb in suitable costumes to play a role? Why?

What about the crazy waterfall, the inverted gravity, the artificial terrain, the eerie blank spots at the ends of hallways, the impossible sun and equally unlikely moon and stars, and the fact that Caleb hadn't aged in twenty-three years? Could all that be achieved by even the most advanced aliens?

"I'll show you," Caleb said with a distinctly sneering look. "What would you like me to make? A person?" His gaze moved to the land speeder behind Liam. "Another one of those? A car? A fire truck?" His face brightened. "What about a TV?"

Despite his doubts, or perhaps because of them, Liam couldn't resist a challenge. "How about making the volcano erupt?"

"Liam," Madison croaked.

Caleb closed his eyes. "Okay, volcano it is."

"We should go," Madison urged in Liam's ear. "Come on."

They both began to edge around the distracted boy, giving him a wide berth, their eyes on the tunnel opening beyond. A whispering sound filled the air, and goosebumps rose on Liam's arms. He ignored the cold feeling and reached for Madison's hand, and together they tiptoed across the dry grass and loose soil as Caleb continued standing there with his eyes firmly shut.

They didn't get far. A sudden roar made them both jump and spin around in fright. The volcano high above was belching black smoke. Seconds later, the top blew off in a dazzling explosion of light. Fireballs shot through the air in all directions, leaving smoky trails as the red-hot projectiles thudded into surrounding fields. As rivers of lava inched down the mountainside, smoke and ash mushroomed across the world and blotted out the sun.

A gloomy darkness descended. Liam and Madison gripped each other tight, staring in amazement and shock. If aliens were watching over this world, if they had hurriedly activated the volcano just to maintain Caleb's delusion of magical power ... then they were deadly serious about this experiment and extremely powerful.

Either that or Caleb really was a magician of the highest caliber.

"That was a good one!" Caleb shouted, jumping up and down. "Best one yet!"

The smog worried Liam. It was approaching fast, a black cloud that threatened to clog his nose and throat, maybe even burn his lungs from the inside. But Caleb didn't seem worried. As the haze arrived and smothered the land all around, the boy stood there and smiled gleefully.

Liam took a few experimental breaths without any ill effects. He turned to Madison, who looked puzzled and scared but otherwise all right. "Why aren't we choking right now?" he demanded.

Caleb shrugged. "Dad said I could only have a volcano if the smoke was safe."

His simple answer, unencumbered by logic, made Liam feel a little better. He breathed easily, struggling to see through the dirty fog. "Okay, fine, you're amazing," he said in a shaky voice. "I don't understand this at all, but it doesn't matter. We're still leaving. You can stay here or come with us, but we're going home. So stand aside!"

He felt like he'd delivered a line in a lavish production of King Arthur, pointing his sword at a group of troublesome peasants and yelling, *I am your king! Stand aside!*

To his surprise, Caleb took a few steps away from the tunnel entrance and nodded. "Go on, then."

Can it really be this easy? Liam wondered. He swallowed and smiled. "Okay. So, are you coming with us, Caleb?"

"No."

Liam nodded. "Fair enough. Well, we'll be back with your dad." He took Madison's hand. "Come on, let's go."

"Not her," Caleb said quietly. "She stays."

Chapter 25

Houston, we have a problem, Liam's inner voice said.

He looked again at the ten-foot-square tunnel entrance. If he shouldered past Caleb and jumped in, he would only tumble for a moment and then simply get up and start running. Madison could easily follow him in. He doubted the boy would come after them.

Then again, the boy didn't *need* to. If Caleb could make a volcano erupt as well as create walking mannequins out of thin air, he could easily collapse a tunnel. He had, after all, brought an entire house down into the ground.

"She has to come with me," Liam said, searching the recesses of his mind for a plausible reason. He let his statement hang to give him a few more seconds.

"Why?" Caleb asked quietly.

"Because."

"Why?"

Nothing came to mind. "Just because!"

"She stays," Caleb muttered, peering meekly through his long hair. "Bring my dad here, and then you can have her back."

His demand took Liam by surprise. "Just come with us," he said at last. "We'll go together."

"I told you, it's not safe up there," Caleb murmured. "The police will get me. I won't go. *You* go. If you really know my dad, which you don't, bring him down here, and then you can have Madison back."

It was almost comical that a boy with such tremendous power could be scared of the police. What would happen if Caleb ran into stern-looking officers? Would he freak out and hurt them? No wonder Barton had run away!—not for his son's protection but everyone else's.

Liam took a quick look around. The distant volcano was silent by now, no longer belching smoke. The black haze had begun to thin. The land speeder hovered nearby, a possible means of escape if the tunnel turned out to be a bust. But where could they go that Caleb couldn't find them? Did his power include some kind of x-ray vision or telepathy that allowed him to know exactly where fugitives were hiding? Liam doubted it, but either way, he had no desire to stick around and find out.

"I'm not leaving without her," Liam said evenly.

"We're walking out together," Madison added for good measure.

Caleb stared at them both for a long time, his gaze flitting from one to the other. Eventually, he folded his arms and shot them a defiant look. "Try it."

Change the subject, Liam thought. *Get him in a better mood. Be his buddy.* "I love the land speeder," he said, jabbing a thumb over his shoulder toward the floating vehicle. "It's so cool. I'm a big *Star Wars* fan. You are too, right?"

"You stole it," Caleb retorted with a glare. "You're a thief. Do you know what I do to thieves?"

Liam shook his head, his stomach lurching. This wasn't quite the reaction he'd hoped for.

"I cut their hands off!" Caleb yelled, making them both jump. "My dad said that in some countries thieves

165

have their hands cut off so they can't steal again. I should cut *your* hands off so *you* can't steal again."

He stuck out his bottom lip and squinted. At first it looked like he was simply pouting, but then the air shimmered and a whispering sound filled the air. He held out his hand, fingers splayed . . . and then yelled triumphantly as a vicious-looking pirate's sword appeared out of nowhere. Its curved, deadly blade glinted even in the hazy air.

"Okay, so you have a sword," Liam murmured, strangely relieved. Of all the things the boy had the power to do, severing limbs with a sword somehow didn't fit. "Go ahead, cut my hands off."

He held his arms out straight. He even turned sideways so Caleb could slash at a convenient angle. Madison backed away, giving Liam a look of disbelief.

Doubt crossed the boy's face. His sword dropped a few inches. He tilted his head and frowned.

"Go ahead," Liam said, his confidence building. "I deserve it. Cut my hands off so I can't steal again. I'll try not to squirt blood all over you. Would you mind bandaging me up afterward so I don't bleed to death?"

The sword lowered another few inches. Now Caleb looked worried. "Bleed to death?" he repeated.

"Sure. That's what'll happen if you cut my hands off—unless you can bandage me up? Maybe put some stitches in?" He screwed up his face, putting on a look of disgust. "It's gonna be really, *really* messy, though. You might want to take your clean shoes off first, or they'll be drenched with hot, sticky blood."

Caleb let the sword drop to his sides. "I'll let you off this time."

Of course you will, Liam thought. He lowered his arms and nodded toward the gaping tunnel entrance. "So we can go?"

The boy rolled his eyes. "I already said *you* can go, but not her."

Liam again considered grabbing Madison's hand and leaping in. Would the boy do anything to them? He might if he were angry enough. Liam feared the young boy's anger more than anything.

But he had to try. Maybe the boy would be too surprised to act.

Before he could talk himself out of it, he grabbed Madison's hand, shoved Caleb in the chest, and hurried past. The boy sprawled in the dirt, his sword flying off to the side as Liam and Madison leapt into the tunnel.

They plunged into darkness, the gas lamps feeble compared to the sunlight. Liam's stomach lurched, and suddenly he was rolling on the dirt-strewn floor, then up on his feet and breaking into a sprint, aware that Madison was right behind him the whole time.

She let out a sudden squeal and gasp.

"Maddy!" Liam yelled, spinning to grab her arm—and missing. She was gone.

Caleb's triumphant yell came from above: "Bungee!"

Just outside the tunnel where daylight flooded in, Madison hung upside down on a long, stretchy cord, bouncing gently. The cord was attached to a wooden tower that hadn't been there half a minute earlier.

Caleb's head and shoulders appeared. "Lights off!" he shouted.

Every single gas lamp fluttered and went out.

"Have fun down there," Caleb said, then disappeared.

Something slammed shut, everything went black, and Liam heard the distinctive click of something metal.

"Maddy!" he yelled again, rushing back down the tunnel and wondering what had happened. It had sounded like a large door with a lock and key, though there hadn't been any such thing moments ago.

Then he paused, hearing something in the darkness behind him. Something big snuffling around farther along the tunnel. Bigger than a Lurker.

Something *really* big.

It hadn't been in the tunnel when he'd first arrived in this crazy world. He held his breath, wishing he could see. Perhaps the creature, whatever it was, didn't know he was there. If he remained quiet and still, it might go away.

So Liam waited.

In his mind, the unseen creature grew more hideous and gigantic with every passing second. At first he imagined a lion because of its lazy, rumbling growl. But when it moved, Liam sensed something much bigger. And it snorted, too, sounding more like a rhinoceros.

It was only when Liam saw a flicker of fire that his nerve broke—the gentle huff of flames from the nostrils of something instantly recognizable.

A dragon.

Liam stifled a moan and stumbled quietly back to the tunnel's end, his arms outstretched, hands groping. He found it at last, something hard and wooden. Where there should have been an opening to daylight, instead a heavy door lay across the tunnel's mouth. *Two* doors, a pair of them. He felt all around, his fingers discovering thick boards, nail heads, and iron straps. They abutted closely, barely a sliver of light between them.

He wanted to yell for Madison but was afraid of attracting the dragon. At the moment, it seemed content to loiter in the darkness some distance away. Caleb must have sent it down to block the way, so maybe it wouldn't attack him . . . but he certainly wouldn't be getting around it anytime soon.

A noise on the other side of the doors caused him to catch his breath. He heard footfalls on the wood, the sounds of fumbling and knocking, a rasping scrape, and something else Liam couldn't identify.

Then a muffled voice from outside. "Liam?"

"Madison!" he whispered.

"Can you hear me?" she called, louder this time.

He winced. "Shh!" he said, rapping his knuckles twice on one of the doors.

Behind him in the darkness, a rumbling growl sounded, and he cowered and prayed Madison would stop trying to talk to him.

"I'm going to get you out!" she yelled. "Caleb walked off and left me here. I guess he thinks I can't open this trapdoor without a key, but he's wrong. Stand back."

Thankfully, silence fell after that. Liam waited.

Then he heard the whine of engines. Madison had started the land speeder. Where was she going?

Its engines roared, but the speeder remained close. Liam imagined Madison circling the tunnel entrance, but he couldn't fathom why. There was another noise, too: a creaking, straining sound. Liam touched the pair of solid doors and felt them shaking.

They flew open with a deafening *crack*. Or one did, anyway. Liam fell backward as the right-hand side swung upward while the left splintered into pieces and fell around him. Daylight flooded into the tunnel.

The roar of the dragon behind him suggested it was annoyed.

The engine faded and cut out. Madison shouted, "Liam!"

He clambered out of the tunnel into blinding sunlight, aware of the thumping footfalls of the dragon as he tumbled forward and fell among the flattened ferns. *Flattened by the dragon*, he thought in a moment of clarity. He heard the roar of flames, and a split second later felt a searing heat coming out of the tunnel behind him.

"Drive!" he yelled as Madison started to climb down from the land speeder. She froze as he stumbled in her direction.

Glancing back, Liam saw a tall, thin, rickety timber structure with a platform at the top, from which the bungee cord dangled. A sturdy wooden frame now existed around the square tunnel opening, and the speeder remained tethered to one of its doors. The thin rope was taut, secured to a wrought-iron handle that clearly wasn't about to come loose.

It took Liam half a second to take all this in as he dashed toward Madison. He knew instantly there was no time to untie the thin rope from the back of the speeder.

"Run!" he yelled.

"Make up your mind," she complained as she jumped down.

With a terrible screech, the dragon exploded from the darkness behind them.

Chapter 26

Again, Liam felt searing heat as flames licked at his rear end. Madison screamed and almost fell, but Liam urged her on, noticing that the back of her t-shirt was smoldering.

He looked over his shoulder as he ran—and then wished he hadn't. He glimpsed the head and neck of a dark-green reptilian monster with a long snout and endless teeth, something he'd seen plenty of times in movies but never, *ever* in his wildest nightmares thought he'd see in real life. It looked like it had been around for some time, one of Caleb's older creations that needed replacing. Some parts of its body were split open, slick with oozing yellow flesh.

The monster was busy squeezing out of the hole, one clawed foot after another, inadvertently scraping more scaly skin from its hide and revealing the slick, yellow flesh beneath. A leathery wing caught on the door frame, and the dragon yanked at it with annoyance. It gave another bellowing screech, and at that point Liam let out a whimper and concentrated on running.

They made it across the fields to the outskirts of the village before the throbbing beat of the dragon's wings overhead made them dart for the cover of a shed, which stood against a stone wall beside a farmhouse. A massive shadow fell across them as Liam frantically rattled the latch and tugged the handle. The small door creaked opened just as another frightening screech filled the air.

They threw themselves into the shed and slammed the door shut.

Gasping, they clung to each other and trembled as the thump of the dragon's wings faded.

"What if it burns the shed down?" Madison whispered.

The thought chilled Liam to the bone, and he cursed himself for being so stupid as to think they were safe. But what else could they have done? Continued running around in open fields?

"Maybe it'll leave us alone," Liam whispered. "Maybe if it can't see us . . ."

Sunlight streamed through various cracks in the flimsy shed walls and bathed them in dusty rays. Liam found gardening tools and bags of seed that had never been opened. There were also several pairs of rubber boots, a few coats hanging on hooks, two rusted buckets, a lantern, cans of paint, spare gate latches and hinges, a shelf full of horseshoes, and a whole load of other objects that Caleb imagined would be stored in a farmer's supply shed. But no axe or shotgun or anything remotely useful as a weapon.

They peered out through the gap in the door. After a while, they spotted the dragon over the fields. It was coming around again. Madison moaned and went huddle in the corner.

The sunlight abruptly switched off.

As before, Liam blurted an exclamation and instinctively reached for the walls, blinking rapidly and trying to find a pinpoint of light to reassure him he hadn't suddenly gone blind.

Madison gripped his arm, making him jump. "There's

no way Caleb's taking a nap right now," she whispered. "He's messing with us."

Liam felt for his flashlight. "I don't suppose you have any double-A batteries, do you?"

"No, but I saw a lantern here somewhere," Madison said.

Liam spun around in the darkness. "That's right. And I have matches." His shaking fingers closed on the box deep within his pocket—flattened but intact. Relieved, he squeezed out a match and struck it. The flame flared, then glowed silently, illuminating Madison's white face in an eerie manner.

The lantern hung on a hook. Inside was a short, fat candle. Liam hurriedly lit the wick and jumped back in surprise when the entire shed lit up in a bright orange glow. "Wow. It really doesn't matter to Caleb how things are *supposed* to work, does it? It's how he *imagines* them to work that's important here."

The candle glowed brighter than it should but otherwise appeared to function normally. Mesmerized, Liam stared at the flame. Its heat melted the wax under the wick, and the vapor rose and burned just as it should. Or did it? Was it real wax? Was its vapor really burning? Or did this imitation candle simply emulate what Caleb had seen in the real world? Where was the distinction between real and pretend if both looked and acted the same way?

He peered over the flame at Madison. "I think the dragon's leaving," she said with her head tilted.

They listened together and eventually heard a distant screech. They both sighed with relief. "And where did Caleb get off to?" Liam asked.

Madison grimaced. "Right after he trapped you in the

173

tunnel, he brushed his hands, said 'Serves him right,' and went off to the village for some chocolate."

"Chocolate? Why?"

"Because he's a kid."

Liam frowned. "So he just left? Without his speeder?"

Madison shrugged. "He left it for me. He said I could catch up with him in the village for some chocolate, or I could sit and sulk."

Liam pushed the shed door open and peered out. The utter blackness had lightened now that the moon was out and stars circled it. "So Caleb's here in the village somewhere?" he said.

"And the dragon's gone," Madison said.

Liam nodded. "All right, then. Time for us to get out of here."

He carried the lantern as they hurried across the field, heading back to the tunnel. The flame danced within the small glass panes, fiercely bright. They hardly needed the lantern now that the moon was at full strength, but they'd certainly need it in the tunnel now that Caleb had doused all the gas lamps.

His heart pounding with excitement, Liam felt they were on their way at last. The land speeder was still there by the tunnel, loosely tethered to the sturdy handle on the busted trap door. The dragon had vanished. Maybe it had landed and resumed its snoozing, hopefully in a distant field somewhere. Liam didn't care as long as it wasn't *here*.

He and Madison peered into the darkness of the tunnel and listened carefully. They waited a full half-minute, barely moving an inch. "Okay," Liam said at last. "It's quiet. I guess the dragon has—"

At that moment, they both clearly heard a rumbling growl from deep within. The sound was all too familiar, and Liam almost yelled with frustration.

Instead, he climbed to his feet and backed slowly away, pulling Madison with him. "It's in there," he mumbled. "I guess Caleb's pet is back on guard duty."

Madison clicked her tongue. "So *now* what?"

With a sigh, Liam turned to face the heavily shrouded village. Only a few lights were on here and there. He suspected it had once been a pretty sight at nighttime—or whatever ridiculous time of the day Caleb turned the sunlight off—but right now it was like a graveyard, silent and almost completely black. "Let's go find Caleb," he said with resignation. "Again."

"And do what?"

"Talk sense into him."

Madison raised an eyebrow. "Good luck with that."

"Do you have a better idea?" Liam demanded.

She considered. "We could drive off in this floating contraption and find another way out. There have to be other ways out, more tunnels leading to the surface. Where else does fresh air come from?"

Liam gestured vaguely. "So we just drive around looking for tunnels buried under ferns and bushes?"

They both gazed up and around. Even in broad daylight, it would be a massive task finding another escape route. *Talk about a needle in a haystack . . .*

"Maybe we can figure out where the drafts are coming from," Madison suggested

Liam licked a finger and held it up.

"All *right*, you win." She sighed. "Shall we use the speeder?"

"Sure."

It took a while to untie the knot from the tail end of the floating vehicle because it had tightened under the strain of tugging on the trap door. When it finally came loose, they tossed the rope down into the grass and climbed aboard.

The speeder had extremely bright beams on the front, as Liam discovered when he flipped a switch marked LIGHTS on the dashboard. They set off across the fields at a steady pace, not because they couldn't see but because it seemed prudent to announce their arrival in an open, non-threatening way, a form of white-flag truce. The last thing they needed was for Caleb to think he was under some kind of attack, otherwise he might conjure up a massive robot from the *Transformers* movies.

Wait—those movies were too new for him. Liam pondered idly as he drove. Maybe something from the 1980s, like one of the *Terminator* cyborgs. He shuddered. He doubted Caleb, who was only eight, had seen the original R-rated movie . . . but still, the idea of being pursued by one of those things gave him the heebie-jeebies.

They joined the paved road and cruised slowly between shop fronts, the beams flooding the street with bright light. The engines merely purred at this leisurely pace. When a small boy stepped out of one of the few brightly lit shops up ahead, Liam brought the land speeder to a halt and shut it off.

"What are *you* doing back here?" the boy shouted. He sounded both annoyed and incredulous. "How did you escape?" Pointing a finger at Madison, he scowled and said, "I *knew* I should have put you in a cage."

He closed his eyes, and a familiar whispering filled the air. A steel cage materialized out of thin air, rectangular and about the size of a small shed. It stood to one side of the road, its door open.

"Get in!" he yelled to Madison.

She raised her voice to be heard the length of the street. "You trapped Liam in the tunnel with a vicious dragon! That was mean, Caleb. Not nice at all. I had to rescue him, otherwise you'd have gotten in *big* trouble with the police."

It was hard to see Caleb's expression from this distance, but he stood still long enough to indicate he was considering her words.

In the end, he sauntered along the road to meet them. One hand was filled with something; he used the other to pop pieces of whatever it was into his mouth. He said nothing until he was just ten feet away, at which point he noisily swallowed his mouthful. "Want a strawberry truffle?" he said, holding out his hand to Madison. His fingers were covered in partially melted chocolate. It smelled good, but Liam felt repulsed.

Madison shook her head. "No. We just want to go home, Caleb. What will it take for you to move your pet dragon?"

Caleb frowned. "Move him where?"

"Out of the tunnel," Liam said. "He's blocking the way."

"Well, he's guarding it," the boy said. "He's *supposed* to be blocking the way. And I won't move him. Ever. Ever *ever* ever."

Chapter 27

Ant gaped in amazement. He'd expected to come across a pile of rubble, the twisted remains of Liam's house scattered throughout the tunnel. Not *this*.

Neatly hung lanterns lit the way ahead, glowing softly as far as he could see. Barton had talked about these. Caleb's elevator had descended half a mile to this exact point. But instead of an old elevator shaft above his head, he saw a massive slab of badly cracked concrete with bits of rebar sticking out. In the center was a small, square hole. And from that hole hung a knotted rope of laundry.

Ant stared for ages, feeling a chill. Faint light came from above, and he could make out the walls of a room as though he were looking up into an attic. Could that be a room in Liam's house? Was he looking up through the underside of the house's foundation?

He must have spent several minutes just standing there gawking. If Barton's story was actually true, Caleb had widened the elevator shaft and allowed the house to fall . . . and yet the tunnel Ant stood in had survived, its walls bracing the entire weight of the house.

Where had all the debris gone? There were definitely signs of a landslide, but it was just a thin layer of rubble across the floor. The vast majority of the displaced rock and earth must have . . . what? Slid off down the tunnel like water running out of a pipe?

Ant finally broke free of his wide-eyed wonder. The rescue crews on the surface had called it a sinkhole, but it was pretty clear to him that a mysterious, supernatural force had caused this so-called natural disaster.

He had to find his friends.

Clambering up the laundry-rope was easy enough. When he pulled himself through the square hole into the room, he let out a sigh of relief. *Liam's laundry room. I'm really here in his house. It survived the fall!*

"Liam!" he shouted, glancing at glow sticks and candles as he hurried from room to room. Though the floor was slanted in places, the walls buckled, and the ceilings low and cracked open, the place was in far better condition than he'd expected. "Where are you? Maddy?"

He quickly concluded he was alone. *Maybe the roof,* he thought hopefully.

His amazement grew when he stepped outside and nearly collided with a cliff face. He raised his lamp to study it, then followed it upward. The eaves were tight against the rock at the corners of the house, but there were big gaps along the sides where he could hoist himself over the gutter and onto the roof. He did so by climbing the drainpipe, the lantern gripped between his teeth. A minute later, he tiptoed to the apex and took in his surroundings.

Nobody here.

Disappointed, he climbed back down and headed back through the house to the laundry room. Once he'd shimmied down the makeshift rope, he turned his attention to the endless array of softly glowing lanterns heading downhill. Liam and Madison must have headed that way, descending toward the world Caleb had created.

He began the trek, knowing he had a long walk ahead.

Caleb's World, he thought with a shiver.

Chapter 28

Caleb crammed the last of the strawberry truffles in his mouth and stood defiantly with chocolate around his mouth and hands on his hips.

"You said I could go," Liam said to him, thinking back to when he and Madison had first met Caleb at the tunnel entrance. The boy had stood aside for him—and only him—to leave. "You told me I could fetch your dad. How was I supposed to do that with a dragon in the way?"

"You weren't," Caleb said, still chewing. "You were supposed to get eaten."

A silence followed.

Caleb licked his lips. "These are so good," he said at last. "Daddy brought some home one time, and I made hundreds of them. They were everywhere—in the kitchen, the living room, the bedroom, even in the bathroom."

He giggled, revealing chocolate-coated teeth.

"Daddy was so mad," Caleb went on. "He said chocolates aren't good for me and told me to get rid of them all. I didn't, though. It's hard to get rid of things."

Liam couldn't help himself. "What do you mean?"

"Well, you know," Caleb said simply, as if the answer was obvious. When Liam merely stared back, Caleb rolled his eyes. "I can make stuff, but I can't *un*make stuff. Once it's made, it's made."

"What about bits that aren't completely made yet?" Liam asked. "Like those black, fuzzy areas in hallways. Those bits aren't made yet, right?"

Caleb nodded. He stared at Liam as if mildly impressed. "Daddy said it's like clay. When I make something like a shop or a car, sometimes I don't bother with the bits nobody can see. That black, cloudy, unfinished stuff is like wet clay. I can fix it later if I want. But the rest of the clay goes hard. Once it's set, I can't change it."

So even Caleb's enormous power had limits. "Is that why you can't . . .*fix* people?" Liam asked tentatively.

Caleb narrowed his eyes. "What do you mean?"

"Well, all these people in your world are deteriorating. Why can't you fix them? Make them better? Make them new again?"

"Because they're *used* already," Caleb snapped. "I just *told* you that. I can't fix them. I can only smash them into a million pieces or melt them into puddles of goo. Don't you listen?"

Liam spread his hands. "I guess I'm still trying to figure it out. I'm not as smart as you, Caleb. Sorry."

Another long silence ensued as the boy nodded thoughtfully and turned to stare at the shop windows. There was absolutely no sign of movement from any of them except *Ming's* a few doors down, where Liam caught sight of the small Chinese woman moving around. Light streamed from the windows, one of the few sources of illumination in the village.

"It's sad, isn't it?" Madison said quietly. "Don't you think? All the shops being empty and dark, I mean."

"Not *all* of them," Caleb said defensively.

"I know, but most of them. All but the food shops are closed now."

Liam nodded and joined in. "I saw a woman with a

181

basket leaving her house to go grocery shopping. Did she get what she wanted? Who does she go home to?"

Caleb said nothing.

Now that he thought about it, Liam couldn't help wondering what happened to all the food that was baked each morning. Or if not baked, then *created*. Whether baked or created, it was good enough to eat or else Caleb wouldn't eat it—and if it was good enough to eat, then surely it had to be capable of rotting. It had to go somewhere, but *where* if nobody came and bought it?

"What happens to old food?" he asked, unable to resist the urge. He had to know.

"It only has a limited shelf life," Caleb said as if repeating something he'd been told a long time ago. "After that it disappears."

An idea struck Liam. "So you *can* make stuff vanish? What about the deteriorating people? Can't you make them disappear?"

Caleb threw up his hands in obvious disgust. "Are you deaf?" he shouted. "I already told you I can't do that!" As if realizing Liam's point, he lowered his voice and added, "Food is different. Daddy said it has a limited shelf life, so I made sure it only lasts a few days."

Liam shook his head in amazement. Every answer the boy offered raised a dozen more questions. The potential for his power went beyond mind-boggling. He had a sudden image of Caleb being spirited away to a secret military base and used to build weapons. Or worse, falling into the hands of the enemy and being used against America. What a terrifying thought!

He suddenly felt burdened with an awful responsibility. He and Madison had to do everything in their power to befriend him. He suspected she'd already figured that out, hence her gentle conversation.

"Doesn't it make you sad, Caleb?" Madison persisted. "Have you ever thought about the future? What will you do? Just stay here alone?"

"That's why I want my dad back," he said sulkily.

"A lot of time has passed by outside," she went on. "Your dad is much older now. He's been waiting for you the whole time, spying on the house you once lived in—where Liam lives now."

"But now we can take you to him, if you'll let us," Liam added.

Caleb rubbed his nose, inadvertently smearing chocolate all over it. His hands were still sticky, and no amount of licking seemed to help. "I could have brought him down here if I'd known where to look. I only knew where the house was."

"Right, but your dad wasn't in it," Madison said quietly, nodding gently. "Maybe you should come with Liam and me to the surface. It's safe as long as we sneak you out and take you straight to your dad."

Liam had to wonder about the wisdom in this plan. Someone like Caleb running around loose? But perhaps Barton should be the one to shoulder the responsibility.

Caleb thought for a moment. Then: "Dad said I could never live on the surface. He said they'd take me away and do horrible experiments on me. Stick *needles* in me."

"Not if you're really, really careful and stay hidden," Madison urged. She bent to look into his eyes. "You look like a perfectly normal and very handsome boy. Nobody would ever know there's something special about you as long as you didn't do any magic."

Caleb blushed at her well-placed compliment. Still, he shook his head. "No, it's not safe. Daddy never let me go anywhere except the lake at the bottom of the lane. I hated being stuck inside the house all the time." He waved his hands expansively. "Here I get to do whatever I want."

Liam felt his patience ebbing. "Well, we can't stay here with you. You get that, right? Madison and I need to leave. Our parents are worried about us. And if we don't show up soon, the police will be heading down that tunnel to find us."

His thinly veiled threat had the desired effect. Caleb's eyes grew round.

"Now," Liam growled, "move that dragon out of the way and let us go!"

For a moment, Caleb's eyes were wide with fright under his hanging hair.

Liam gripped the boy's shoulders and stared hard at him. "I'm not going to lie to you, Caleb. You have the power to do whatever you want to me. But I'm not going to stick around here, and nor is Madison. We're leaving through that tunnel. You're invited to come with us—or you can stay here alone. I hope you decide to come, but only you can make that choice."

He stepped back. Caleb looked confused.

"Your dad is up there on the surface," Liam said, jabbing his thumb upward. "We can take you to him."

A silence stretched between them. Caleb was obviously deep in thought.

"Yes or no?" Liam prompted.

Still Caleb seemed undecided.

Liam threw up his hands and turned away. "Okay, Madison and I are leaving now. If the dragon's still guarding that tunnel . . . well, then I guess it'll eat us both alive. It's up to you, Caleb. I hope you'll do the right thing."

Without another word, he and Madison climbed into the land speeder. Liam powered it up and carefully turned the vehicle all the way around until the bright beams washed over the eight-year-old. Caleb blinked furiously in the glare.

"See you, Caleb," Liam said over the hum of the engines. Receiving no reply, he sped away down the street.

As they left the paved road and headed across the fields with the dazzling beams bouncing off ugly bushes and wizened trees, Madison sighed and said, "Think he'll get rid of the dragon?"

"No idea. Honestly, I don't even know how he controls it. Or *if* he controls it."

The beams picked out their escape route—a black hole at the foot of the flimsy-looking bungee tower. One of the broken trap doors still hung from its hinges, partially obscuring the squared-off frame that surrounded the tunnel opening. Liam kept expecting the dragon to leap out and blast them with fire.

"The dragon's probably still in there," he murmured.

"Let's wait a bit," Madison said. "Maybe Caleb will ask it to leave."

"How? With telepathy?"

"Funny enough, I find that really easy to believe."

Leaving the lights on full, Liam climbed down from the land speeder. "Let's hide behind that tree over there."

They waited in silence, hidden in the darkness. High above, the twinkling stars lazily circled the moon like meteoric debris around Saturn. It was a detail that bore little relation to actual science; this was pure childish imagination. Still, it was extremely pretty and certainly beat the planetarium Liam had visited with his class a few years back.

A noise caught his attention. It came not from the tunnel ahead but from somewhere off to his left. He swung around, squinting in the glare of the speeder's beams.

The noise came again, a faint rustling in the grass. And another several yards away.

Shadows moved into view—shambling, stumbling figures closing in from all around. Liam let out a moan.

Lurkers.

Chapter 29

"Run," Liam whispered to Madison. "To the tunnel!"

"The *tunnel*? But the dragon—"

He understood her reluctance, but as twenty or more Lurkers came stumbling in from all around, the framed tunnel entrance became their only possible alternative. Even the land speeder was out of their reach now; two Lurkers came around the side, flinching as they moved into the glare of its beams.

The tunnel. Maybe the dragon won't hear us . . .

He and Madison made a dash for the square, black hole in the ground. Lurkers came after them, their moans and pants filling the air. Glancing back, Liam saw them silhouetted against the land speeder's blinding lights, several shadows converging into a single mass, a clumsy but relentless mob.

"What do they *want* with us?" he gasped as they arrived at the tunnel.

Before Madison could answer, a thunderous roar stopped them in their tracks. A burst of flame shot straight up out of the square hole, hot and blinding, causing Lurkers to rear backward with their arms shielding their faces. Liam stumbled against the flimsy tower and absently clutched at the bungee cord to steady himself.

The dragon's snout appeared. With a bellow, it began to struggle out of the tight space, squeezing its bulk through the wooden frame. The remaining door held fast, wide open and lying flat against the grass.

"We're dead," Liam moaned.

The dragon seemed to be having trouble this time, though. The frame restricted its movements. It had squeezed out earlier, then back in again, but this time its wing had snagged, and it lacked the gumption to back up and try again. It grew angrier with every thrust, fire licking from its mouth.

Liam and Madison retreated—into the path of stumbling Lurkers, who rushed forward, clutching and grabbing. Madison screamed as she was pulled away, and Liam yelled in terror as the weight of multiple bodies pressed in. Then his shouts caught in his throat as the reek of rotting onions made him gag repeatedly. The mob pushed him this way and that, and abruptly Liam went down amid grasping hands.

The dragon roared again. The Lurkers either didn't notice or didn't care. Liam couldn't decide if he'd rather die in a blast of fire or at the putrid hands of an angry mob. He gasped as the weight of the Lurkers threatened to squeeze the life out of him. A boot clubbed him in the ear, and a knee dug into his shoulder.

With every passing second, he marveled that these zombified monsters had not yet begun the process of pulling off his limbs, clawing out his intestines, and chewing on his brain like they did in movies. He decided he'd rather have the dragon end it all quickly. Anything but *this*.

The dragon continued its frantic struggles, rumbling and snapping in fury. But those frenzied noises, along with the moans of Liam's attackers, became a distant murmur compared to the sound of his thudding heart and gasping breaths.

Meanwhile, Madison yelled angrily the whole time.

The idea of being outdone by a girl sent a jolt through him. He was *Liam Mackenzie*, the boy who couldn't die! He'd survived far worse than a bunch of walking mannequins and a dragon too fat and stupid to escape from its lair!

He scowled, suddenly clear-headed as he peered up at his assailants. Since these monsters were unable to form coherent sentences with their creepy lipless mouths, they merely grunted and moaned. Liam recognized a word here and there but couldn't make out what they were trying to say. The main thing was that they weren't trying to kill him. They weren't even trying to hurt him.

Something pressed into his right hand. A balled-up piece of paper.

Astonishment settled over him as the Lurkers gently lifted him to his feet. His legs were so shaky that his knees buckled repeatedly. He swayed and tried to compose himself as a sea of ugly melting faces danced before him. Beyond, the dragon paused, panting hard. It ducked down, disappearing from sight.

"Liam?"

Although Madison sounded a million miles away, her voice cut through the chorus of unintelligible moans as Lurkers nudged her into view. She looked disheveled but unharmed, a puzzled frown on her face. She joined Liam, and they stood there together as the circle closed around them.

"What . . . ?" Liam croaked. His throat and lips were dry from his own ragged panting. He licked his lips and swallowed. "What's all this about?"

"Look and see," Madison urged, peering with interest

at the balled-up paper clutched in his hand. He'd been holding it aloft as though it were a prize.

Blinking, Liam looked around the shadowed faces, seeing half-melted skin and white skulls, bulging eyeballs as well as eyeless sockets, eerie lipless grins, and more than a few missing limbs. The stench hit him again. He turned in a circle, confirming that he was surrounded by a wall of jostling figures.

They fell silent and waited expectantly, obviously wanting Liam to look at the paper. With one hand, he smoothed the paper against his belly and peered at it. Stained and crumpled, it smelled of fish and chips, possibly stolen from *Ming's*, or more likely retrieved from a trashcan. Words were scrawled across it in untidy handwriting, the writing smudged but perfectly legible:

help us die

At first Liam thought the word "or" was missing. Surely it should read *help us or die*. That made much more sense where these hideous monsters were concerned.

But, slowly, the true meaning surfaced in his addled brain. *Help us die.* These creatures were slowly melting, becoming less mobile as feet broke off or legs twisted and buckled. Some of them were blind, stumbling around in perpetual darkness, keenly aware of their gradual demise.

He looked at Madison. "They're becoming self aware," he whispered.

She nodded sagely.

What a terrible notion—that these poor Lurkers were growing smarter while their bodies deteriorated! Liam tried to imagine what it must be like to wake from a hazy but relatively happy dream only to find his skin sloughing off and his limbs rotting away. What kind of life could these poor souls look forward to? And Caleb refused to destroy them.

Liam's fear and disgust evaporated. Now he felt nothing but pity. Of *course* he and Madison had to help them. Who else would? Certainly not Caleb.

In a flash, Liam remembered the puddle of nastiness on the rocks at the foot of the waterfall. Madison had suggested the Lurker had fallen, but perhaps it had been an attempt at suicide. Had it been successful? Had the rotting mannequin's pseudo-life ceased the moment his head smashed open on the rocks?

Well, duh, he thought. *If it had died, it would still be there.*

So it hadn't hit the ground hard enough? It had only dented its head instead of cracking it open? How horrible.

Liam looked from one grotesque face to another. He couldn't bear ask them how he could help them die, so he modified his question slightly. "How can we help?"

Two words came back, repeated in unison by all, surprisingly clear:

Kill usssss . . .

Madison closed her eyes, and a tear broke free and rolled down her cheek.

"But how?" Liam asked shakily, hardly able to believe he was even having this conversation. There was no way he could kill them, and he knew it. No wonder Caleb had been unable to. A responsible adult could do it if there was no other choice, like shooting a severely injured horse to put it out of its misery. But Liam was certain he couldn't do it. Not *this*. And a young boy like Caleb certainly couldn't. The thought of *murdering* these people, even at their request, made him break out in a sweat.

Thankfully, the conversation ended abruptly when the sun flared into life, blinding and hot. Liam and Madison staggered and shielded their faces, aware that the Lurkers were screaming and throwing themselves onto the ground.

Liam blinked in the blinding sunlight as heat warmed his skin. He squinted and watched with horror as, all around, dozens of Lurkers huddled on the grass trying to protect their eyes. Faint wisps of smoke rose from their shoulders. The smell of rotting onions sharpened. Many of the creatures jerked to their feet and staggered off across the field toward the village in what Liam guessed was an urgent dash for the darkness of shops.

Six others had the sense to head for more obvious cover nearby—the tunnel. But none of them made it, because the dragon burst forth with a terrible screech, splintering the sturdy timber frame and rattling the half-door that still hung from it. The Lurkers crumpled to the grass as the massive reptilian tore loose and clambered out. It reared up and bellowed, dark green and shiny in the glaring sunlight.

As the creatures cowered there at its feet, great chunks of yellowed flesh slid off their faces and arms. The faint wisps of smoke rising from their shoulders turned into thick, black, acrid fumes. There were no flames, just a lot of smoke. Waxy flesh sizzled and bubbled, and more lumps slid off foreheads and cheeks to land with heavy splats in the grass. At this stage of deterioration, evidently the sun's rays were deadly to these non-living human facsimiles.

"This is horrible," Liam muttered. He tried to move, but his feet refused to acknowledge the command from his brain.

Four other Lurkers lay in the grass a short distance away, clearly conscious but equally incapable of moving. In their case, it was because their limbs were too far gone. Or simply because they lacked the will.

Death by sunlight, Liam thought. It reminded him of the way vampires exploded into flame—except these imitation people were simply melting. How long would it take them to expire? Did it really hurt? And what exactly would kill them in the end? Would they still be alive even after their flesh had entirely melted away? He imagined them lying helplessly in the long grass, nothing but glistening skeletal figures held together only with Caleb's imagination and perhaps rudimentary ligaments and muscles.

Madison tugged at his sleeve. "Liam! Why are you standing here gawking? Let's go!"

He tore his gaze from the Lurkers and shook himself. She was right. The dragon hadn't given up its guard duty yet, but it might attack at any moment.

He turned to run . . .

. . . and spotted Caleb hurrying toward them across the field, his face red with anger. "You're not going *anywhere* until you prove you know my dad!"

Chapter 30

Liam looked at Madison, wondering how they were supposed to provide evidence that they knew Barton. She looked as exasperated as he felt.

The eight-year-old boy came trotting up. Circling around, he passed under the dragon's snout as it stood there huffing plumes of steam. He faced Liam. "Well? Show me proof."

"How am I supposed to do that?"

Caleb shrugged. "Tell me something about him."

Thinking hard, Liam said, "Um, kind of a thin face, beak nose, wrinkles around his eyes, thin grey hair—"

"Sounds nothing like him."

"Well, he's older now."

Madison broke in. "He's a chauffeur. Drives a big limousine. Does that help?"

This made Caleb scoff with disgust. "Nope."

"He talked about you," Liam said, eyeing the dragon and wondering again if he and Madison could somehow dart past it. "He told us . . . uh . . ."

"Told you what?"

The truth was, Barton hadn't said much at all, certainly not to Liam. He decided to try a different tactic, one that might buy him a little time. "You know what? I'm not saying anything until you clean up your mess."

Caleb's eyes widened. "My . . . *mess?*"

"These poor people," he said firmly. "There's no way your dad will take you back until you sort this out."

"Huh?"

Madison jumped in. "You can't leave them like this. It's cruel."

She pointed to the nearest Lurker as it finally stopped writhing. It was hunched into a ball with its face turned toward them. One eye was missing, but the other was big and staring. It had no eyelids, nor most of its face on that side; it looked like a skull with bright yellow butter smeared over it in random dabs. The flesh was shiny and moist, running freely into the grass. With a strange sucking sound, the creature's left arm came loose at the shoulder beneath the filthy long-sleeved shirt. If the Lurker stood up, the arm would likely slip right out of its sleeve and fall with a plop to the ground.

"You have to fix this," Liam said quietly. Treading softly might be better than a stern approach as far as Caleb was concerned. "And then we'll talk about your dad."

Caleb sniffed and wrinkled his nose. "You want me to put him down," he said flatly, looking at the badly deteriorated Lurker.

"Not just him. All of them. You've got to put things right around here. You can't just leave them all here to . . . to suffer like this. You have to do something."

"I can't. I already told you I can't *fix* things. I can only make *new* things."

"Caleb—" Madison started.

Liam stepped closer to the boy, doing his best to control his trembling anger. "You said you could destroy things you've made. You used to put these people down when they started deteriorating, right?"

"Dad always made me," Caleb said sullenly. "I didn't like it."

Liam took a deep breath. He told himself it wasn't the boy's fault. He was just an eight-year-old kid, after all. "I get it, Caleb. It's a nasty business. But it's even nastier leaving them to suffer like this." He looked down, realizing that he still held the wrinkled piece of paper the Lurkers had given him. He held it out so Caleb could read it. "Look. They *wrote* this, see? They're asking me to help them *die*."

Caleb stared at the message, then looked away. "Do it, then. Help them die."

Now Liam felt weak. It was no good asking an eight-year-old boy to murder a bunch of dying, suffering people—fake or otherwise—if he wasn't prepared to do it himself. And he knew he couldn't.

"I don't know how," he said, spreading his hands. "*How* do they die? Do they have hearts and brains?"

Caleb scoffed. "Of *course* not. Daddy said not to give them hearts and brains. Their heads are full of mush."

"Well, they're pretty smart for brainless imbeciles," Liam muttered.

Madison leaned closer to Caleb. "What can you come up with that's . . . that's quick and painless?"

Caleb shrugged. "A bomb? Or a gigantic alien disintegrating laser?" He thought for a moment. "Being buried under tons of rock should squish them dead. Or being eaten by my pet dragon. Or burned by my pet dragon's super-hot fire-breath—"

"Stop," Liam ordered. "This isn't funny."

The eight-year-old let out a sigh. "Do you want to leave or not?"

Liam shook his head and folded his arms. "Not until you deal with this problem. And deal with it properly."

196

"How am I supposed to do that?" Caleb yelled. "Most of them have run away! They could be anywhere! It'll take ages to find 'em all now. And then there's a bunch of 'em in the garage back at my house—Whoops." He clapped his hand over his mouth.

"I know about them," Liam said. "And you need to deal with them, too."

"But—"

"Figure it out, Caleb. You're not seeing your dad until you do."

The boy threw up his hands and gave an exclamation of disgust. He stormed off, then changed direction and began stomping toward his dragon—and then, to Liam's relief, changed direction again and ended up pacing aimlessly back and forth, muttering under his breath.

"Cannonball!" he yelled suddenly. He had a furious expression as he pointed toward the one-armed Lurker. It seemed to be aware it was the subject of Caleb's attention, and it swiveled a single eyeball to look at him.

"What—?" Liam started to say.

But he got no further because a massive iron ball the size of a small car whistled through the air from above. It smashed deep into the ground, taking the Lurker with it. The impact showered Liam with dirt and almost threw him off his feet. He gasped and staggered. A crater had opened up, much wider than the iron ball itself. The Lurker had disappeared entirely, utterly pulverized.

"That did it," Caleb said, turning to glare at Liam. "Or how about . . ." He scratched his nose, and Liam barely had time to register the faint shimmering in the air before the boy turned and pointed at another Lurker. "Giant Jaws of Death!" he screamed.

The ground immediately surrounding the quivering Lurker rumbled and opened up to reveal a set of enormous molars spanning six feet. The Lurker dropped into the gaping maw, and the jaws clashed together. There was a terrible cracking sound, and Liam saw a squirt of yellow from one side of the giant mouth. The long grass thrashed to and fro as the monster beneath the ground chewed vigorously, then swallowed.

Horrified, Liam fell to his knees. "Caleb, no—"

"What's wrong?" the boy snapped. "You wanted me to kill them, didn't you?"

He stomped over to a third Lurker. There were only two left in this area; another six still huddled in front of the dragon. All of them had become oddly quiet by now as if anticipating their impending deaths. More than that, Liam sensed a *longing*.

The chosen victim reached for Caleb as he approached. Acrid smoke billowed out of its filthy sleeve, and the boy stopped and waved his hand around to clear the air. "Okay, for you I think I'll use the giant laser gun from space."

The fact that there was no visible sky in this world seemed irrelevant to Caleb as he squinted and concentrated. Liam saw the telltale ripple in the air. "Caleb, please, not like this! There has to be a better way."

A blinding flash of red light burst from the direction of the sun and incinerated the Lurker. It was certainly effective—the creature's legs and waist turned to ash in a split second, and Liam was reminded of the Gorvian time grubs he'd encountered last weekend. As the ray of death faded, some of the ash blew away in the draft from the nearby tunnel. Unfortunately, the ray had only taken out half the Lurker; the remaining half remained alive and unharmed. It let out a low, mournful wail.

"Caleb!" Liam yelled.

"No problem, I've got this," the boy muttered.

The bright red column of light flashed again, this time incinerating the top half of the Lurker. Liam blinked rapidly and sidled over, amazement overcoming his fear and disgust. The two separate blasts of light had left a section of blackened grass shaped like a number 8. It was filled with gray ash and nothing more.

Madison had her hands over her face. "There has to be a better way," she murmured.

"How?" Caleb complained. He gestured all around. "There's only seven left here. Most have run off to the village to hide. And what about the ones in the garage near my house? They're *everywhere*." He stomped a foot in the dirt, looking more like a petulant child than ever before. "Maybe I should just drop a few bombs! I don't care about it anymore. I don't care if the whole *world* is flattened. I might as well—"

He paused to digest his own words, and a look of intense excitement came over his face as he raised his eyes and stared all around. A terrible sense of dread filled Liam. The boy was contemplating something *big*.

Quietly, Liam began to edge toward the tunnel, pulling Madison with him. The dragon continued to lie there, now half asleep, but the idea of going near those massive jaws paled in comparison to sticking around and witnessing whatever Caleb did next.

"We need to go," he whispered to Madison. "Right *now*."

Chapter 31

Liam and Madison sidled closer to the dragon, both keenly aware of its sleepy but baleful stare. Up close, however, the monster somehow didn't seem quite as authentic with its oddly regular scales and bright-white teeth and claws. Like a giant animated model, it looked a little too perfect to be the real deal.

Well, duh, Liam thought. *It's a dragon, a creature from myth and legend.*

It stank of onions. Yellow slime dribbled down its flanks from open wounds where it had torn its way out of the tunnel.

Still, the creature wasn't so far gone that it couldn't rise up and bite him in half without a moment's hesitation, and it probably would have done so already if Caleb hadn't been around. Like a highly trained guard dog, the dragon glared with suspicion and sniffed with disdain as they tiptoed past. Obviously waiting for an instruction, its muscles tightened, and enormous claws dug into the dirt. The slightest nod from Caleb was all it needed to strike.

But Caleb was busy.

Liam and Madison edged past the dragon toward the tunnel. The pit of darkness still had half a trap door hanging from the side, attached only by a single sturdy hinge. Tied to the door's wrought-iron handle, a thin rope lay in the long grass, recently untied from the speeder. Liam stepped over it, his eyes on the tunnel. "What's Caleb doing back there?" he whispered.

"I don't know," Madison answered him, looking over her shoulder. "He's mumbling. The air is shimmering."

"That's a bad sign."

Madison paused, her eyes narrowed. "I've never seen the air shimmer so much before."

Trying to ignore the dragon, Liam turned to look. An ever-widening ripple distorted his view of the terrain. The village shimmered like a reflection in a pond. The distant hills wobbled, and the upside-down world above their heads jiggled.

An odd tingling sensation crept up Liam's fingers to his shoulders, then across his chest. Even the dragon seemed to be aware of something strange, and it lifted its head and sniffed the air. "Let's go," Liam urged.

Without warning, he shoved Madison over the tunnel's timber threshold. She gave a yelp and tumbled down inside.

Liam prepared to jump—but first, he glanced back at Caleb.

An intense feeling of dizziness washed over him.

"Whoa!" he gasped as he tilted backward and scrabbled for something to hold onto.

At the same time, Caleb gave a shrill giggle and tore past him. The boy was moving so fast that he seemed to fly into the tunnel with a tremendous bound, leaving Liam to fall on his rear end in the flattened ferns.

The dragon hauled itself to its feet, sniffing the air and growling. Then it flapped its wings and took off, rising rapidly and soaring away. Something had spooked it.

Liam swayed, his sense of balance inexplicably screwed up—and he hadn't even entered the tunnel yet. He ended up on hands and knees as an unseen force threatened to tug him away from the trap door. Glancing up, he stared in amazement at the tall, rickety bungee tower the dragon had been sleeping next to. The stretchy cord was slowly being dragged by the same unseen force that tugged on Liam. Like the hand of a clock that had been on the six, the cord slowly rose to the right until it reached the five . . . then the four . . .

He suddenly figured it out.

Caleb had switched off the gravity.

Abruptly, Liam lost his balance again and started rolling helplessly across the field in the direction of the village. *Rolling down a steep hill*, he thought in a panic. Without Caleb's false gravity, the ground literally tilted under him as Earth's true gravity took hold. He was dimly aware of Lurkers tumbling with him. One fell apart, limbs and chunks of yellow flesh flying off in all directions. The land speeder spun away out of control.

Liam yelled in panic, grabbing at the long grass as he tumbled.

The rope! It still lay in the grass to his right. He lunged and gripped it with both hands, quickly arresting his fall.

Suddenly, his senses rebooted and everything clarified. The grassy field he'd walked across earlier was slowly becoming a sheer cliff face. The tunnel entrance now lay *above* him, an opening in the side of Caleb's world, and Liam dangled on a rope still attached to the wrought-iron handle of the busted trap door.

He swung from side to side, hanging on for dear life.

The bungee tower stuck out sideways, its cord also hanging straight down. The village he'd explored appeared to be fixed to the side of the curving landscape below, the structures collapsing as he gawked in amazement.

"Climb!" Madison screamed from above.

With his arms aching, Liam scanned the grassy wall above and spotted Madison peering over the edge of the wooden frame, her head and shoulders poking out of the tunnel. Her black hair hung down toward him as she glanced around in wide-eyed shock.

"Climb!" she screamed again. "You've got to hurry! Caleb turned off the gravity!"

No kidding, he thought.

Anything she yelled after that was drowned out by a rising cacophony of cracks and rumbles from all around.

Chapter 32

Ant froze as the tunnel began to shake. Dust trickled down on him. He felt sure the entire place was about to cave in and crush him, and there was absolutely nothing he could do about it. And yet . . .

Was that light ahead?

It had been an unnerving journey. He'd walked for ages in the light of endless gas lamps. Then they'd inexplicably snuffed out, and he'd fumbled to switch on his own battery-powered lantern, grateful he'd brought it. He'd heard distant rumbling sounds echoing along the tunnel, followed by occasional unearthly screeches. The urge to turn and head back up the tunnel had almost overpowered him, but the thought of his friends in danger forced him onward down the gentle slope, grinding his teeth together and trying to control his thudding heart.

And now this. An earthquake? Another sinkhole?

The light he saw ahead had nothing to do with gas lamps. This was a square of white daylight. The earthquake—or whatever it was—rumbled up the tunnel toward him, and he again fought the urge to flee.

A shriek caused him to gasp, and he almost dropped his lantern. The shriek came again, and this time he recognized the voice.

Madison!

He broke into a run, stumbling over the loose rubble and occasional bits of twisted metal. What had she been yelling? It had sounded like "Climb!" and then something else he couldn't make out. In any case, she had to be yelling to Liam.

"I'm coming!" Ant yelled, but the increasing roar drowned out his words.

As he drew near to the square of light, he saw two figures silhouetted there. One of them was clearly Madison, but the other looked too small to be Liam.

"Maddy!" he called, stumbling as another massive shudder hammered the tunnel.

He closed the gap, shouting the whole time, and finally Madison swung to face him. He still couldn't see her face against the blinding light beyond, but it was definitely her.

She let out a gasp as he threw himself down next to her. "A-Ant? W-what are you—?"

Her words seemed like a distant murmur compared to the booms of whatever catastrophic disaster was occurring outside. He was only vaguely aware of the small boy kneeling next to him. *Caleb*, he guessed as he tried to hold on to the shaking ground, grasping loose rocks in his clawlike hands and trying to block out the terrible din. Though he knelt shoulder to shoulder with Barton's powerful son, all he could think about right now was the mind-blowing scale of destruction unfolding before his eyes.

He leaned forward to get a better look. The tunnel opened out on the side of a cliff, a deadly drop if he were to tumble out. But far below, the cliff curved away in a rolling expanse of countryside. And it kept on curving away, starting to rise again in the distance, up and up, higher and higher, until . . .

It took only moments to figure out that he was, almost

literally, an ant on the inside wall of a gigantic sphere miles across. *Caleb's World.* He looked down on a picturesque scene of fields and forests, but the beauty was quickly decimated by falling earth and rubble as the landscape came unstuck from the upper half of the sphere. In the center of it all, a massive fireball had embedded itself in the ground, its crater steadily blackening around the edges, fire spreading outward.

He watched, stunned, as entire forests—thousands of trees together with the soil and rock they were rooted to—literally peeled loose of the sphere's ceiling and fell in slow motion toward the fields below. The colossal cloud of debris hammered down in what had to be the deadliest downpour in history, millions of tons of trees and rock and earth turning the lower landscape into mush.

A single upside-down mountain, what looked like a hanging volcano, cracked apart around its base and unleashed further doom and destruction. For a second or two, it fell almost in one giant chunk . . . but then it split apart in eerie slow motion. As the gargantuan sections fell, bright-orange lava rained down amid billowing black smoke.

"Help Liam!" Madison screamed at the small boy. "Help him!"

Caleb shrugged. "Too late."

Ant tore his gaze from the destruction and blinked at her. "Where *is* Liam?" he yelled.

She pointed downward, a frantic look on her face.

Ant leaned out again, acutely aware of the deluge of soil pouring like a muddy waterfall just a yard from his face. Rocks the size of his fist and boulders as big as cows tumbled past, and he gasped with terror.

Liam was not far below, hanging off a rope in the middle of the avalanche. He kept squeezing his eyes shut because of the cascading dirt, but it was a miracle nothing bigger had swept him away. He was climbing at a snail's pace.

Ant followed the rope up. It was tethered to the remains of a half-door hanging from its hinges to one side of the tunnel opening. Fearful of being hit by the cascading debris right in front of his nose, he reached for the taut rope and tried pulling on it, but he wasn't strong enough to hoist his friend up.

While Madison wore a stricken, tear-stained expression, Caleb had a wide-eyed look of wonder. Ant crawled closer to the boy and shouted in his face. "Your dad sent me to get you! He's waiting for you outside!"

Caleb scowled. "Liar. That's what the others said."

"It's true!" Ant dug in his pocket and pulled out his phone. He thumbed his way to the photo gallery and twisted the screen around so Caleb could see. "See? There's your dad and me."

Precious seconds ticked past as Caleb stared at the screen. The thunderous racket increased, and out of the corner of his eye, Ant saw flashes of explosions as the massive fireball embedded in the distant field ignited the grass all around.

Caleb's mouth fell open. After a while, he looked at Ant and shouted, "He's really outside?"

Ant stuffed his phone back in his pocket and grabbed the boy's shirt. "Help Liam NOW!"

Chapter 33

Liam glanced left and right. On the vertical faces of the world to both sides, the grassy terrain tore loose, sliding off in clumps of dirt and turf. Some of it came from higher up where the walls leaned inward, showering the back of Madison's head. She gave a squeal and ducked inside the tunnel, only to reappear a second later to yell some more at Liam, who was too busy being pelted with clods of grass and small rocks to hear what she was saying.

He climbed, one hand after another, fighting the urge to look down but blinking too furiously to look up. The rope seemed a mile long, and he knew he had very little time before he was wiped off the side of the cliff by far heavier cascading debris.

Yet he paused again, unable to believe what he was seeing all around.

The sun finally relented to normalized gravity and plummeted, slamming down in a field just beyond the English village and leaving a crater that quickly blackened. Flames leapt into the air.

The village itself, now on a slant, seemed intact until rocks rained down, smashing through rooftops and shattering windows. Loose soil showered the land all around, slowly darkening the lush grass.

Gasping with amazement, Liam thrashed about on the rope, trying to climb while gawking at the spectacle.

Far above, the world was literally falling apart. The sand dune he had crossed not so long ago erupted into a massive yellow cloud. Endless grassy hills crumbled and rained down. Thousands of trees in numerous forests shook loose and began to plummet, twisting and tumbling.

With ear-splitting booms, the volcano cracked apart around its base and started to fall in gargantuan chunks. Rivers of lava fell like bright-orange ribbons. When it all finally slammed down a few miles below, giant chunks of mountainside shattered and spread outward along with sprays of lava, and the once-beautiful countryside was burned and smothered in an instant.

Much of the sphere's ceiling was bare by this time, having spilled millions of tons of rock in frightening slow motion. Now cracks appeared, spreading quickly, and it seemed the entire planet was about to fall apart . . .

"CLIMB!" Madison screamed once more.

Liam broke free of his open-mouthed paralysis and resumed his struggle, finding strength he never knew he had, one hand over the other, left, right, left, right. *I can't die, I can't die*, he told himself the whole time. But he knew he wouldn't make it, not with all this debris pouring down in his face. It was all he could do to snatch glances here and there. He felt sure that the larger boulders were missing him by inches. Maybe they were. Maybe the universe was nudging them away, trying to prevent his death yet again.

The tall, rickety bungee tower abruptly fell away. More clods of earth spattered his head and shoulders. A wave of intense heat swept over him as the fallen sun flared brighter and set the surrounding fields alight.

Just when Liam thought an avalanche would wipe him off the side of the world, he heard a screech from below and instinctively looked down. The dragon was there, beating its massive wings as it tried to escape the carnage. Rocks slammed down on it, and it spun out of sight. But it returned moments later, dodging the largest boulders and fighting through the rest, rising fast toward Liam, its eyes fixed on him.

Just what I need, Liam thought in horror. *The end of the world isn't enough. Caleb has to send his pet dragon after me as well!*

The monster shot upward and gripped him hard around the waist with one giant paw, pinning his arms to his sides. Its leathery wings shielded him for the next few seconds as it continued ascending, and Liam was able to keep his eyes open and get a good look at everything—at the dirt and rocks pounding the dragon's body from above, the slowly blackening sky all around, the flashes of explosions from what had once been the sun . . .

Globs of yellow flesh spattered his face and clothes as the dragon took a severe beating from the deadly cascading rock. The creature was knocked senseless, its upward flight cut off—but then it tossed Liam away, and he flew through the air toward the cliff. He had a split second to see the square opening in the wall before he tumbled into the darkness of the tunnel.

He landed roughly, and by the time he'd turned around to look back outside, the dragon was long gone. Liam saw nothing but a choking deluge as Caleb's World vanished forever.

Hands pulled at him. "You're safe now," Madison gasped as he struggled to sit up. "Caleb made his dragon help."

Liam caught final glimpses of the collapsing world— images that he would never forget, especially the blazing sun as it lay in a smoldering heap on the blackened hills, a colossal ball of fire that continued to burn even as forests and houses and earth rained down on it.

Then came suffocating darkness.

* * *

Everything fell silent.

A blinding light caused Liam to yell and jerk backward, certain a fiery ball was about to incinerate him. But it was just the beam from the miner's helmet Caleb was wearing.

Dazed, Liam did a double take. "Where did you find that?" He shook his head. "Never mind. What's wrong with relighting the gas lamps on the walls?"

"This is more fun," Caleb said happily, rapping his knuckles on the hard hat.

Liam rubbed his eyes and looked around. He must have been out of it for a few seconds, because he had no recollection of the transition from deafening noise to this welcoming silence. Madison knelt opposite him, a disheveled mess covered in a fine layer of dust. And next to her . . .

"What the—?" he exclaimed. "*Ant?* How—why—?"

Ant grinned. "Couldn't let you have all the fun."

Both Liam and Madison stared at him until his smile faded.

"I found a back way in," Ant explained. "Barton showed me. We got in ahead of the rescue workers." He frowned. "Speaking of which, we should probably head back. We need to sneak Caleb out of this place before anyone sees him. Let's go."

Liam slowly climbed to his feet and studied the floor-to-ceiling pile of rocks that now blocked the way into Caleb's World. The roof fall had only just missed them, but it had acted as a shield against the destructive force of the recent catastrophic event. On the other side of that thick wall, a wondrous place had existed until just minutes ago. Now? Nothing but a staggering amount of mess. Soil and rock and trees and houses and vehicles and—

And Lurkers.

He grimaced. He guessed Caleb's demolition had done the job perfectly. He'd switched off the gravity, and now everything was gone. Every last trace of his crazy world was buried, leaving only the massive underground chamber itself, perfectly round, an anomaly in the Earth's crust. If rescue workers found their way down here and dug through this roof fall and into that enormous, partially filled spherical void . . .

Madison patted his hand. "Let's get out of here."

"Yeah," Caleb said, jiggling his helmet from side to side. He scowled at Ant. "Take me to my dad."

Ant scowled back. "Ask nicely."

Liam used his hand to block the glare of Caleb's dazzling lamp. "And turn the lights back on, please."

Caleb sighed and closed his eyes. Seconds later, every gas lamp in the tunnel flickered into life. He kept his helmet switched on, though.

Liam took once last look at the roof fall, then turned to peer up the sloping tunnel. *The way out.* He pushed past Ant and started marching.

He couldn't help noticing that Ant wrinkled his nose. "Man, you need a shower," his friend said. "You too, Maddy. Not attractive."

"Okay, so we stink," she retorted. "We've done a lot of running around, escaping monsters and stuff. What's *your* excuse?"

He laughed.

Liam turned back. "Ant, what are you even doing down here? I thought Madison's message was pretty clear about you staying away."

"Yeah," Madison griped. "What part of 'stay away' don't you understand? I didn't sleep-write that instruction for nothing."

"Good thing I didn't listen, or Liam would be buried in Earth's core by now."

"We're nowhere near the core," Liam muttered.

Ant ignored him. "The way I see it, your message said to stay clear of the house *as it was sinking into the ground*. It didn't say anything about afterward."

After a pause, Madison said, "I'm now wondering if there was another reason I told you to stay outside. If you hadn't stayed with Barton, then he never would have showed you a back way into these tunnels, and you wouldn't have arrived in the nick of time and did what we couldn't—shown Caleb proof that we're friends of his dad."

"Where *is* Barton?" Liam asked.

"He couldn't come," Ant said. "Caleb banished him from the tunnel ages ago. Anyone can enter except him."

Liam waited for a more detailed explanation of this mysterious statement, but none came. Caleb seemed to understand, though, judging by the sheepish look on his face.

"I'd be dead by now if that dragon hadn't given me a boost," Liam said, his thoughts returning to his close escape. All that falling debris and spatters of lava . . . Suddenly angry, he reached out and punched Caleb hard on the arm despite the inherent danger of provoking a boy with incredible powers.

"Ow!" Caleb yelled, swinging around. "Don't you DARE—"

Ant stepped between them, his hands outstretched. "Enough! Caleb, settle down or I'll tell your dad what a brat you've been. Everybody's safe, and that's all that matters right now." He turned to face Liam. "Right?"

"Right," he mumbled.

Madison rolled her eyes. "When you boys have finished squabbling, can we please get out of this place?"

Chapter 34

The uphill trek was tiring. It didn't help that the ground was so soft and lumpy, a thick carpet of loose soil and rubble mingled with twisted bits of metal.

"What *is* this?" Liam wondered aloud, kicking at it and stubbing his toe.

"Elevator," Caleb said.

His cryptic response begged an explanation, but Liam was too tired to care.

Caleb led the way, talking loudly about how the tunnel stretched all the way to the surface, thus confirming Ant's all-too-brief explanation. "It's a really long way, though," he warned. "We need something to ride in. How about I make us—"

"Walking is fine," Madison said sternly.

Ant stayed by Caleb's side, talking quietly to him, obviously trying to keep the peace, even showing him the picture of Barton again. The boy's eyes widened, a grin spreading across his face. "He looks so old," he squawked.

Liam lagged behind with Madison, holding hands to help each other over the uneven, treacherous rubble. They talked for a while but then fell silent. Liam was too busy thinking about what came next, and he was sure Madison was just as worried. Could they really unleash someone as powerful as Caleb on the world?

For the next fifteen minutes, the only sounds were their footfalls in the dirt, heavy breathing, and the occasional rumbles far behind. Now that the tunnel was blocked, the draft was gone and the air still. With everything that had happened lately—the endless walking, the heart-pounding terror of being chased by hideous creatures, the anxiety and tension brought on by facing Caleb, the collapse of his impossible world, and now the intense relief at being on his way home—Liam felt ready to drop. He couldn't wait for a good hot bath and then bed. He would sleep for days.

But of course he had no bed anymore. He had no home to go to.

He sighed, too exhausted to wonder where he and his family would end up for the foreseeable future. Maybe Ant's house? It didn't really matter as long as he had a bath and a bed. Maybe Caleb could conjure up—

He shuddered. *No way.*

When Madison stumbled and her grip on his hand tightened, Liam thanked the universe for saving them both. No wonder her future self had warned Ant away in her sleep-written message. He might have died several times over! But maybe she was right and Ant's primary purpose had always been to find a back way in so that Caleb could be snuck out without anyone seeing him.

The boy turned to face them, the beam on his helmet dazzling. "My feet are tired. I'm going to get us something to ride in. How about a—"

"No!" Liam said sharply. He let go of Madison's hand and stamped toward Caleb, blinking in the glare. "No more of your magic. Don't you understand yet? You have to stop. If you want to fit into the real world up there, you have to be careful." He softened his voice. "Look, I'm not saying you should *completely* stop using your magic. Just use it sparingly, you know? When you really need it."

"Actually," Ant said, putting a hand on Caleb's shoulder and looking at Liam, "it wouldn't be a bad idea to speed things up a little, you know? Those rescue workers could arrive any minute. This is a really long walk, and—"

Liam shook his head firmly. "No."

Ant shrugged, a sign of reluctant agreement.

Caleb looked thoughtful as he stared at the tunnel floor. Eventually he looked up again, and Liam winced as the beam shone directly in his face. "Not even a tiny flying saucer?"

"Especially not that," Madison said.

They resumed their weary march.

After a minute or two, Liam said, "A flying saucer?"

"Liam," Madison whispered.

Caleb stopped and grinned. "Yeah, a little one, just big enough to fit inside. It'll be shiny and round, and it'll float along really fast."

Madison shook her head firmly. "We don't need your magic."

But Liam stared at Ant, and he stared back. A flicker of excitement lit up his friend's eyes. "What do you think, Ant?"

"This *is* a long walk. We should get Caleb to the surface as fast possible—"

"NO!" Madison shouted, making them all jump. She clenched and unclenched her fists and glared at both Liam and Ant in turn. "Enough! Let's keep walking."

Nothing more was said as they continued their journey. The uphill trek went on and on, and Caleb complained countless times about his sore feet. Out of respect for Madison, Liam sided with her and flatly told the boy to quit whining, and to his surprise, Caleb refrained. *Just needs a firm hand*, he thought.

Eventually, Caleb gave an excited cry and turned to dazzle them again with his miner's lamp. "My house! I really *did* bring it down, didn't I?"

Liam ground his teeth together. "You sure did."

It was hard to feel anything but relief at the sight of the weird protrusion sticking down from the ceiling, a massive chunk of rock that spanned the width of the tunnel and stretched fifty feet or so. It was here that the gas lamps petered out. Darkness lay beyond. But in the center of the ceiling, a small hole led up into the laundry room.

"We're here," Liam said with relief. "Wait," he said, lowering his voice to a whisper. "Did I just see a light move up there?"

He hurried past Madison and clambered up the garment rope. It smelled faintly of Lurker. When he emerged in the laundry room, he found soft light emanating from the hallway and kitchen as expected—the glow sticks and candles he'd laid out around the house— but what really caught his interest was the hard white light bobbing around in the living room.

He sensed movement behind him and swung around to find Madison on her way up. "Someone's here," he whispered. "Probably rescue workers."

"Good timing," she said with a hint of sarcasm. "Now that we don't need rescuing . . ."

They both hurried back down the rope. Liam noticed some of the knots were tiny, probably impossible to untie now. He also heard a slight rip from somewhere. And again, that awful lingering onion smell.

He faced Ant and Caleb, once more squinting in the glare of the boy's headlamp. "They're here. Maddy and me will go up and meet them while you two carry on up the tunnel."

Madison frowned. "And then what? Barton can't hide him forever. Are you sure we can't find some way for Caleb to just go home to his dad and live normally?"

Liam mimicked writing in a notebook. He frowned, deepened his voice, and took a stab at how the police interview would go: "What's your name again, sir? Barton? Hmm, I can't find you anywhere in the system. Can you prove this boy is yours? Wait, now you're saying Barton isn't your real name? Then what is? . . . Ah, now I can find your records. But wait on a minute—there's a long-standing warrant out for your arrest! You're a fugitive, missing for the past twenty-three years! And you *still* can't prove this is your son. Yes, the records do show you have a son, sir, but he's in his early thirties now. Hmm, that's strange. His name was Caleb, too. There's something funny going on here. Are you right in the head, sir? Perhaps you need to see a psychiatrist . . ."

Madison batted his arm. "All right, enough."

Liam tucked his imaginary notebook in an imaginary shirt pocket. "All right, Caleb, you go on out with Ant. Go find your dad. Maybe we'll see you again soon. Don't do anything crazy, okay?"

"I won't," Caleb said meekly.

Ant nudged him. "Let's go. See you soon, guys and gals."

He and Caleb headed off, trudging up the tunnel into darkness, no longer accompanied by an endless array of gas lamps. Only the beam of the helmet lit their way.

Liam sighed. "We're done, Maddy. Come on."

They climbed up into the laundry room and stepped carefully into the hallway. The candle on the floor burned silently, a puddle of wax in its center. The white light came from the living room, and Liam headed that way with Madison at his side.

"Hey, about time you showed," he said loudly to the rescue worker that stood there.

Chapter 35

Ant burned with curiosity. Was everything Barton had said about his son true? Could he really conjure things from thin air?

He'd glimpsed Caleb's strange world in its final moments, so there was no doubt of its existence. But had a mere boy really created it? A dragon had flashed by the tunnel opening and thrown Liam to safety just in time, but again, where was the proof Caleb had been instrumental in that? Back on the surface, Barton had told a lot of fantastic stories and revealed a weird illusory wall that he alone couldn't penetrate. Ant had walked along a perfectly square tunnel supposedly created by an eight-year-old boy, and he'd witnessed the death of a hideous melting man. Despite all that, he still found it hard to believe a mere kid could conjure stuff out of thin air.

He looked back. The light of the gas lamps had faded into the distance. Soon, rescue workers would be lowering themselves into the tunnel and flashing their bright beams around. Hopefully they'd head downhill first, curious about the lamps.

"Hey, Caleb?" he said.

"Yeah?"

"You mentioned something about a flying saucer . . ."

Caleb stopped and shone his helmet light directly into Ant's face. "Yeah! Can I make one?"

Ant nodded. "Just keep it between us, okay? And make it without lights, otherwise we might be seen. This isn't *Close Encounters of the Third Kind*. Go subtle, all right? No lights."

Grinning, Caleb closed his eyes, his lips moving.

Ant took a few steps backward as a sinister whispering sound filled the tunnel. He turned to look behind him and saw nothing. When he turned to the front again, he almost fell over in surprise.

Floating two feet off the ground was a disk-shaped silver vehicle about eight feet in diameter, with a glass dome on top. *A tiny flying saucer*, he thought incredulously. *No way!*

The light from his lantern and Caleb's helmet bounced off the saucer's reflective surface and illuminated the tunnel further. It positively glowed.

"Martian spaceship," Caleb said happily. "I made it with two seats, see?"

The glass dome slid back, and Ant moved closer. Sure enough, a pair of seats awaited them. The one on the right had a steering wheel in front of it. Caleb scrambled up onto the smooth, rounded surface and caused the craft to tilt alarmingly. He climbed into the driver seat and switched off his helmet. "Come on!" he yelled.

Fighting to control his shock, Ant gripped the side of the saucer. "Move over," he ordered.

Caleb complained but slid sideways.

Ant felt like he was in dream. He was actually boarding a *flying saucer*. Okay, so not a true alien ship made by aliens from another world, but a super-advanced spacecraft all the same, hovering in a way that no Earth-constructed machine could. Whether it could survive the rigors of space was another matter—and one that he didn't want to test.

When the glass canopy closed over their heads and Ant nudged the steering wheel forward, dozens of external lights came on, and the ship punched forward. Ant gripped the steering wheel and watched the tunnel speed by in a dazzling, colorful array of color. With only eighteen inches of clearance on either side, it was hard to keep it from hitting the walls, but it didn't seem to matter much; it just scraped and caused a shower of sparks. Despite everything Barton had told him about this boy, only now did Ant appreciate the sheer power being wielded—by an eight-year-old.

It was terrifying.

Ant's long, slow walk down the tunnel to the fallen house had taken an hour or more. The journey back to the surface took just a few minutes. He was glad to get past the sticky yellow mess that had once been a walking, talking mannequin.

When he reached the end of the tunnel, he slowed the craft and approached cautiously. And after nudging the rounded the saucer outside into the moonlight, he looked back to find the mountainside as solid as ever. He stopped amid the trees, and the glass dome slid back as though smart enough to anticipate his intention to deboard.

The craft was too wide to slip between the trees, but it would be safe to leave it here for now. He jumped down. "Your dad is here somewhere. Come on."

Caleb looked unsure as he flipped a few switches and dimmed the saucer's external lighting, and he took his time climbing down, the hovering craft wobbling like a boat in water.

It was at that moment Barton appeared from the trees. "My son," he said, his voice breaking.

Caleb swung around, and his face lit up. "Daddy!"

He practically leapt into his father's arms and hung there as Barton gripped him tight and swayed from side to side, mumbling something in his ear. With a lump in his throat, Ant watched as his normally stoic driver dissolved into a weeping mess. When he finally put Caleb down, he sank to his knees and seemed weak, drained of energy, wiping his eyes and tugging his son close again.

"I missed you, Daddy," Caleb said loudly, his voice cutting sharply through the night. "I tried to make another you, but it fell apart just like the rest."

Barton visibly winced at the boy's statement, but he nodded and tried to smile. "Nothing like the real thing, huh? But we're together again now. It's time to move on."

Caleb studied him. "You look old. You're all wrinkly and grey."

"I *am* old, son. You kept me waiting a long time. Twenty-three years, to be exact."

The boy's mouth fell open. "Sorry."

"And you don't look a day older than you were when I left you," Barton added, his voice tinged with wonder. "You really did stay young."

"I made time speed by outside."

Barton raised an eyebrow. "Or you slowed time inside. I suppose it's the same thing. How long do *you* think I've been gone?"

Caleb thought about this with a look of great concentration on his face. "I don't know. Weeks and weeks and weeks."

"How many people have deteriorated?"

"Most of them. I replaced a few. But it's all gone now. All blown up. I turned off the gravity." He let out a giggle and clapped a hand over his mouth.

Ant couldn't help thinking the boy's manner was overly immature for an eight-year-old. But then, he hadn't had a lot of interaction with anyone but his dad throughout his life. Probably most of what he'd learned about real life had come from the TV.

Barton patted Caleb's shoulder and climbed to his feet. "We'll talk later. Let's get Ant home, and then we'll be off. But first . . ." He stood and pondered, looking toward the smooth cliff face. "You know, a vast tunnel is strange but not supernaturally bizarre. I'm not too worried about anyone finding it. Let them puzzle over it for years. However, the illusion needs to go. Caleb?"

"What?"

"Please remove the illusion. Open up the tunnel. Let people find it, as I'm sure they will now. They'll assume it was an old, unfinished mine. When they wander up this way and come out here, I don't want them to find a magical wall."

"Oh, okay," Caleb said. He closed his eyes and frowned. Abruptly, a ten-foot-square section of the cliff faded away, leaving a black opening.

"And turn the gas lamps off," Ant advised. "Nobody will believe Liam and Maddy lit all those things themselves."

"Lights out!" Caleb yelled, then grinned. "It's dark now."

Barton studied the flying saucer with great interest before leading the way through the trees toward the waiting limousine.

As the three of them walked, Ant said, "Where are you two planning to go?"

"Yeah, Dad, where are we going?"

"Well, that little spacecraft back there might be very useful," Barton said. "Perhaps we'll give it a spin and get far away from here. We'll go someplace where nobody will ask questions about me. I'll have to test out the ship's capabilities, maybe head straight upward above the clouds, then zip around the Earth . . ."

"We could go to the moon!" Caleb shouted.

His dad shook his head. "No. There's no TV on the moon, son. Everybody knows that."

"Oh." Caleb thought for a moment. "But I could *make* TV work on the moon—"

"No. We're staying on Earth. And you're going to be a good boy and listen to me this time," he added sternly. "Right?"

Caleb hung his head. "Yes, Dad."

"So another state?" Ant asked.

"A bit farther than that, Master Anthony," Barton said. "England, perhaps. We'll retire to a small village somewhere."

Caleb looked disappointed. "Sounds boring."

They emerged by the lane, and Barton unlocked the car. He winked at Ant as he opened the front passenger door. "One final ride, my friend. I'll take you home, and then I'll come back for the tiny spaceship in the woods."

"Are you leaving me here?" Caleb said, his voice rising in panic.

"Not a chance. You're riding in the back. But you must stay out of sight."

As Barton climbed into the driver's seat and Caleb flung himself into the spacious rear, Ant sighed and knew it had to be this way. Taking care of the all-powerful and incredibly dangerous boy was Barton's job, and he couldn't do it here in a town where people knew him, where the authorities knew him as a middle-aged man with no family. They needed to go away together. Far, far away.

"One final ride," Barton said again as he buckled his seatbelt and looked sideways at Ant. "Where to, my friend?"

"Madison's house."

Barton allowed a faint smile. "Right away, Master Anthony."

Ant shook his head as the reality truly sunk in. "This means you're not going to be my driver anymore."

"Correct. This little jaunt will be our last."

"But . . . but who will—?"

"I'm sure your father will find someone better suited to the task than me."

Ant said nothing. No Barton? It didn't seem right.

Things would never be the same again.

Chapter 36

Liam and Madison stood on the roof of the house with a rescue worker who called himself PJ. Wearing a helmet similar to Caleb's, with a bright light on top, he'd come down ahead of the others as an advance scout. He'd sent his rope back up, and now others were arriving.

Together, they watched as four more figures silently descended the shaft, winched down from equipment high above, all hanging off one long tether at intervals. They landed one by one, each stepping aside to clear the way.

Now the warped rooftop seemed very crowded. PJ, along with two other men and two women, stamped around talking about how perfectly the house fit into the circular shaft. "It's in such good shape!" one man commented.

PJ said, "This is Liam Mackenzie. And the other is Madison Parker."

"Safe and sound," one of the women said. She spoke softly into a walkie-talkie that had a wire of its own, connecting it directly to the surface instead of relying on a weak or nonexistent underground signal. "We got them. Both kids are alive and well. Repeat, alive and well."

A burst of static followed, then a tinny voice: "Roger that."

PJ was probably in his fifties with heavy eyebrows and a goatee. He had the look of someone with decades of experience in this line of work. Although fierce-looking, he also had a kind twinkle in his eye and a grin of white, even teeth. He'd already been exploring the house when Liam and Madison had met him. Now, as he prepared to descend for a full inspection, he winked at Liam and said loudly, "Looks like these kids have been partying down there. They trashed the house."

"It wasn't my fault," Liam said.

"It was totally his fault," Madison assured the man.

All the rescue workers laughed in unison, and Liam felt a great weight lifting. Everything was going to be all right.

"Well, let's get you kids to the surface. Plenty of time for talking later. Come on."

* * *

Liam felt like a deteriorating Lurker, barely able to stand. He just wanted to sleep. One of the rescuers kept offering him and Madison bottles of water while another checked their faces and prodded them gently. They seemed almost overly protective, asking over and over what injuries they'd sustained. "Any broken bones? Sprains? Gashes?" Liam had a few minor bumps, but he played them down. He was too tired to care.

Not much was required of them for the journey to the surface. Two men attached a harness to Liam and fastened it, and then the walkie-talkie woman ordered someone on the surface to "bring him up." As he lifted into the air, he looked down and watched as they fitted Madison with a similar harness. She left the rooftop moments later, attached to the same rope—one very, very long rope. A man rose with them, while PJ and the others stayed behind to explore.

The ascent was painfully slow. Liam couldn't help dozing off, and he woke to a circle of daylight above. *Not daylight*, he reminded himself. *It's still the middle of the night.* Whatever dazzling array of searchlights they'd set up, he saw the heads and shoulders of people silhouetted around the rim. The rope was attached to a winch fixed to a sturdy framework standing across the fifty-foot shaft.

"We're here," Liam said.

Madison jerked awake. "Huh?"

"Wake up, sleepyhead."

As soon as fresh air hit him, a scream went up. He heard the words, "My baby! My BABY!"

Inwardly, Liam groaned and wished his mom would tone it down just a little bit. But he couldn't help choking up when he saw her ashen face and tear-streaked cheeks. Workers pulled him to one side of the shaft and grabbed him tightly while they unfastened the harness. Then he swayed and staggered into her arms.

She was babbling in his ear, but he barely made out her words. Then his dad rushed over and almost knocked him and his mom down.

He gasped at the masses of people running about on the lawn at this late hour—mostly firefighters, medics, and police officers, but a good number of neighbors as well. He lost sight of Madison in the crowd, but she was around somewhere, being jostled and hugged and cried all over.

One person was missing: his best friend Ant. He kept one eye on the lane while trying his best to answer a barrage of questions from his dad. "Are you hurt? What happened down there? How were you not crushed? Did you find flashlights okay? Did you feel that tremor a little while ago? First a sinkhole, then an earthquake . . ."

Oh, you mean Caleb's world collapsing? "Yep."

Medics kept trying to interrupt the reunion, gesturing toward an ambulance parked on the grass and saying he should get a check-up. But his mom held him tight, and his dad waved them off, saying, "In a minute!"

Liam spotted Madison with a grey blanket around her shoulders, her parents leading her toward the same ambulance, Cody ambling by their side. He decided now might, after all, be a good time for a checkup, and he led his parents over, still amazed at how many strangers milled about on the lawn. He noticed a news van in the lane, too. He guessed it was a pretty big story, a house sinking into the ground like that. This would be the second time his family had featured on the local news; the first time had been just a couple of weekends ago when the Ark Lord's yellow stasis cloud had descended on the house and a plethora of monsters had run amuck and torn the place up.

Now the house was gone, just a huge, gaping hole in the ground. *Like it was vaporized*, he thought. *Ant's vision came true.*

He vowed to pay attention to echoes of the future from now on. The scene had played out exactly as foreseen; only Ant's interpretation of it had been different.

"Looks like we'll be pitching tents from now on," Liam said to Madison as he joined her and the medics at the back of the ambulance. Both sets of parents crowded around.

"You'll be staying with us," her mom, Mrs. Parker, said firmly.

"We can't impose," Liam's dad said. "We need to figure out something a bit more permanent. We'll check into a nearby hotel. I think the insurance will pay for it, at least for a while."

"What are you going to do with *this*?" Mr. Parker asked, gesturing toward the lawn. It was as if small-talk and chit-chat had been suspended throughout the entire ordeal, only resuming now that Liam and Madison were back safe and sound. "It's not like a hole that size can be filled in with a bit of gravel."

"We'll worry about it later. I'm just happy both kids are okay. The house . . ." He shrugged. "Maybe I'll rebuild somewhere else on the lawn and cover the hole."

Mr. Parker looked doubtful. "If they let you. Inspectors will be out here poking around, checking to see if the area is safe, worrying about more sinkholes . . . Heck, *we* might be told to vacate the premises as well." He put his arm around his wife. "Can you face another move?"

Madison's mom grimaced. "We just got here. Please don't let them tear our house down."

"They won't," Liam said, thinking of his visit to the future. Now that he thought about it, he couldn't be sure whether his own house had ever been rebuilt. What he *did* know was that Madison's would remained unchanged. It was where the two of them would live until a ripe old age.

He couldn't reveal any of this, though. He reddened as everyone looked at him.

"Well, as long as you're sure, Liam," Mrs. Parker said with a laugh.

The rescue workers who had remained below were now full-fledged explorers. Liam imagined them picking their way through the house, eventually finding the hole in the laundry room floor, then heading down the tunnel.

They would walk for some time before coming to a blockage. Would they try to dig through? Maybe eventually, in the days to come . . . and when they did, they'd find a massive, three-mile-wide spherical void.

And if they walked *up* the tunnel, which they definitely would, they would emerge in the woods as Ant and Caleb must have done by now. The whole place would be a hive of activity for months, perhaps years, as they tried to figure out who had built the tunnel and where the hundreds of gas lamps had come from.

Liam couldn't help smiling.

Madison nudged Liam and pointed toward the lane. A dozen people loitered there behind the yellow CAUTION tape despite it being just past 4 AM, and some turned to watch as a black limousine slowed to a halt behind them. Ant stepped out of the front end and quickly closed the door, then turned back as the window slid down. He leaned it and talked for a moment, then stepped away and waved as the window rolled up.

The limo moved on toward the lake, and Ant watched it go, his shoulders slumped. After a while, he turned toward the lawn, where a police officer politely stopped him from crossing the yellow tape.

"Can someone let him through?" Madison said. She broke free of her mom's grasp. "Come on, Liam, let's rescue him."

* * *

"My dad'll buy you a new house," Ant said, gesturing toward the enormous hole in the ground.

Now that the rescue was over, all the focus was on the

233

so-called sinkhole. What had caused it? What else was down there? More to the point, what would they think of the partially melted mannequin in the upper half of the tunnel?

Ant suddenly looked embarrassed at what he'd said. "When I say my dad'll buy you a new house, I mean if your dad's insurance doesn't cover it, and if he'll accept a helping hand . . ."

Liam wasn't worried. "It'll work out," he said. "I'm more interested in Caleb. And Barton, too. He's really gone for good?"

"Didn't even hand in his notice," Ant said glumly. "He's probably already left in that flying saucer. They're going to England. Let's hope Caleb behaves himself."

"So . . . does this mean you won't have a driver now?" Liam wondered aloud. How would Ant get around without a chauffeur? Pay for a taxi?

"Oh, I'm sure my dad will replace him pretty quick. It's just that . . . well, Barton was cool. A new driver might not turn a blind eye to all the weird stuff we get involved in. We'll have to be more careful. We'll have to watch what we say."

After a silence, Madison said, "Maybe I just need to stop sleep writing. It used to be harmless fun, watching aliens poke around in fields in the middle of the night. Since meeting you guys, it's gotten way too dangerous."

Ant glared at her. "Don't you *dare* stop sleep writing."

"She won't," Liam said with a grin. "If there's one thing I'm sure of, it's that we're gonna have a bunch more dangerous adventures together."

A SNEAK PEEK AT THE NEXT BOOK IN
THE SLEEP WRITER SERIES . . .

A slice of dazzling white light appeared, hanging in the air like a bolt of lightning frozen in time. Then it widened, opening up into a circular wormhole, its surface rippling like water on a pond before sucking inward and forming a swirling tunnel.

But a tunnel to where?

Liam peeked at his phone. 4:04 PM, right on time. Madison had done it again, predicting the event with uncanny precision. *Nothing uncanny about it*, he reminded himself, thinking of future-Madison and her time-traveling ways. She'd known precisely when this would happen.

"Well, this beats watching a movie," he whispered.

"Depends what's coming," Ant replied.

Madison grimaced. "I'm hoping something harmless this time. I've had enough of nasty monsters."

They watched in silence, waiting to see what would emerge from the wormhole. When a tiny, distant figure appeared, they ducked lower and peered through the bushes without moving a muscle. Liam couldn't help wondering if they shouldn't have distanced themselves a bit more. What if these aliens carried heat-detecting equipment to warn of nearby life forms? And what if they were armed with brain-melting ray guns?

In *Warp Giants* (Sleep Writer Book 4), an alien visitor takes Liam, Ant, and Madison on a journey they will never forget—to a distant planet quite unlike Earth where a species of massive beasts faces extinction.

But will the travelers be home in time for supper?

OTHER SCI-FI AND FANTASY NOVELS
BY THE SAME AUTHOR

In *Island of Fog*, a group of twelve-year-old children have never seen the world beyond the fog, never seen a blue sky or felt the warmth of the sun on their skin. And now they're starting to change into monsters! What is the secret behind the mysterious fog? Who is the stranger that shows up one morning, and where did she come from?

Hal Franklin and his friends are determined to uncover the truth about their newfound shapeshifting abilities, and their quest takes them to the forbidden lighthouse . . .

There are nine books in this series, plus a number of short stories available for free at islandoffog.com. It's an expansive saga set in a parallel Earth with plenty of magic and familiar creatures from myth and legend.

Also look for a spin-off series set twenty years in the future and starring a new generation of shapeshifters.

In *Fractured*, the world of Apparatum is divided. To the west lies the high-tech city of Apparati, governed by a corrupt mayor and his brutal military general. To the east, spread around the mountains and forests, the seven enclaves of Apparata are ruled by an overbearing sovereign and his evil chancellor. Between them lies the Ruins, or the Broken Lands—all that's left of a sprawling civilization before it fractured. Hundreds of years have passed, and neither world knows the other exists.

Until now.

We follow Kyle and Logan on their journey of discovery. Laws are harsh. In the city, Kyle's tech implant fails to work, rendering him worthless in the eyes of the mayor. In the enclaves, Logan is unable to tether to any of the spirits, and he is deemed an outcast. Facing execution, the two young fugitives escape their homes and set out into the wastelands to forge a new life. But their destinies are intertwined, for the separate worlds of Apparati and Apparata are two faces of the same coin . . . and it turns out that everyone has a twin.

There are two books in this series, with a third (a prequel) planned for the future. This series is co-written with author Brian Clopper.

In *Quincy's Curse*, poor Quincy Flack is cursed with terrible luck. After losing his parents and later his uncle and aunt in a series of freak accidents, Megan Mugwood is a little worried about befriending him when he moves into the village of Ramshackle Bottom. But word has it that incredibly good fortune shines on him sometimes, too. Indeed, it turns out that he found a bag of valuable treasure in the woods just a few months ago! As luck would have it, Megan has chosen the worst possible time to be around him.

This is a fantasy for all ages, a complex and rewarding tale, a little dark in places but also a lot of fun.

Go to **UnearthlyTales.com** for more information.